A
MIST SPRITE'S
STUDY
OF BEING
HUMAN

A Mist Sprite's Study of Being Human
by Kyra Hinton

Paperback published by Mosslings Press May 2025

First edition.

ISBN: 979-8-9911085-0-8

Illustrations by Sara Willia and Kyra Hinton
Editing by Becky Sweeney

Here's to the poets, who cannot be silenced,
who remind us of the places,
we cannot return.

THIS IS HOW THE STORY GOES

I MARGIE

Margie and the Glen   1

Margie and the Headless Pine   8

Margie and the Land Breakers   12

Margie and the Songs   17

Margie and the Burning Ones   24

Margie and the Broken Tongues   32

Margie and the Ones Who Stayed   37

Margie and the Leanabh a' Cheo   44

II AILA + MARGIE

The Child and the Mist   53

The Mist and the Garden   62

The Child and the Bones   74

The Mist and the Flames   83

The Child and the Basket   91

The Mist and the Salt Air   101

The Child and the Sea   112

The Mist and the Villages   123

III THE MIST

The Mist in the Stone Garden   133
The Mist Along the Paths   142
The Mist Within the Ruins   146
The Mist Over the Waters   150
The Mist Amidst the Heather   154
The Mist Beside the Mushrooms   158
The Mist Within the Trees   162
The Mist Atop the Heights   166

Epilogue   174
Historical References   182
Bibliography   190
Author's Note   194
Acknowledgments   200

I

Margie

Margie and the Glen

On a day just like any other (mind you, this is Margie's very favorite sort of day) she found herself floating towards the Old Wood. Floating, because she didn't have a body, and the Old Wood because it just felt right. It was an Old Wood sort of day.

There was a decayed log down there, a rotten thing that had become very dear to Margie. This very normal, any old day seemed the perfect time to pay it a visit. On and on through the Old Wood Margie's misty form whirled and dipped, below branches and 'round moss-capped stones. A few of these little fellows had replaced their green caps for purple ones of heather. Margie gave those an extra pat as she drifted past.

The log for which Margie aimed was a normal sort of log. Quite right; the very kind. A magical genus, were those 'normal' sorts. This one had become Margie's favorite for the very reason of its everyday, garden-variety shape (I swear she'd tell you this herself, if she were able to, and knew what a garden was).

There was another reason Margie believed today a perfect day for a log-visit. Her dear forest and hills and burrows and falls had been extra water-kissed for the last few sun visits. If her study of place had taught her one thing (and she'd learned far more than one thing, just as any eternal being made of non-corporeal mist would have, given the time, but there is one fact particularly pertinent to this moment) then it was this: watery skies make logs wet. And, when logs are wet...

"Mushrooms!" Margie would have cried, had she a voice. Instead, the wind picked up her sentiment and the dripping drops of water plopped in tune so her exclamation came out as a sort of *whoosh pitter plop*. You might, if you were in the Old Woods that day, have thought it a very normal, everyday forest sound. And, trust me, Margie would gladly have accepted the compliment. But you are not in the woods. Margie is, and, with a grand exclamation of *whoosh pitter plop*, she found her mushrooms.

Floating fast as fog, Margie giddily approached the mushrooms and settled gently, as a human might lean on elbows, to take a closer look. Her joy rushed through her fragile form like a huffed breath on a cold morning and kissed the frilled edge of the nearest mushroom. Margie condensed some of her self into a tiny dew drop and rolled across the dimpled, spongey cap. She navigated around a deep pockmark of the slightly nibbled form, until she hung as a droplet from the fringe of the very edge. Before gravity could have its way, Margie studied the gills beneath, memorizing the way they wove and split. From here, they reminded her of the patterns in the river.

Plop!

With the most natural exclamation, Margie-as-droplet landed on the upturned moss and loam which had kindly made room for the mushroom's recent emergence. She let her moisture spread

and spread until she seeped down deep enough into the soil to feel the branching mycelium that made up the fungi's true, beating heart. Margie soaked in the vibrating pulse of the water pumping through the soil, as more fruiting bodies prepared for their brief stint above ground.

With a sigh like a gentle breeze lifting the corner of a fallen leaf, Margie pulled this drop of her self back to the surface, back into the air where she split into the cool mist kissing the floor of the Old Wood. From here she observed the lichen's progress as it spread across the log's surface, punctuated intermittently by shelves for snails to rest upon and mossy tendrils to climb.

If she could, Margie would have grinned at the everyday magic of this garden-variety log on a normal day like this one. She might even giggle, and the sound would be like wing beats of startled birds taking flight. But as she can neither giggle nor grin and so, when you hear the sound of the birds, it is likely only that: frightened birds on a normal day in the Old Wood.

It's okay if that makes you sad. It might make Margie sad, too, if she knew the feeling.

But Margie was not feeling sad. For while we might grieve for the eternal being who cannot grin or giggle, she was distracted by the river's roar from the valley below. She busied herself thinking of the way its twists were mirrored in the underbelly of her new favorite mushroom. When she sprang up and up, the movement licked up tendrils of mist to kiss the red bark of the pines growing in the cover of their elders.

Margie followed the sound of her sister waters who burble on calm days and rage on others. This was a rage day, the roar of the falls wild as it drew her in. The spray moistened the rocks and grasses along the flooded edges, and Margie was lost to it, mingling through it and flowing down with a sound that felt like wingbeats.

When the water crashed into the rocky base of the falls she billowed and gathered back into herself, soft like the clouds on the clearer days.

If she had the lips to do so, she'd have smiled at the wildness of the wind, and the thrill of the world in this brief space suspended before the fall. Instead Margie gathered some of her drops together and released them in a spit of rain to further kiss the magic of the ground below. You might, if you were by the falls that day, wonder if the drizzle were the tears of a being who knows not how to cry.

For eons Margie has inhabited the space just above the ground, her body a misty kiss upon unruly Highland grasses. So, when she fell back to her place, did it take minutes or hours? Does time apply to the eternal? Does mist make a sound if no one is in the glen to hear it fall? Wait, no, that's not the saying. It's no matter. After an untold amount of time, Margie fell back to the earth and flattened herself to the soil she's cared for longer than you've known how to read the words I am saying to you now.

Odd, isn't it, to think there are things truer than time? Things that have lived, and moved, and inhabited a place long enough to watch it change beneath their feet. (I'm using 'feet' here purely as a turn of phrase. Mist has no feet.)

When you think of an eternal being formed of a naturally occurring, everyday phenomena, perhaps you imagine an aged, wise, graying man. Ageist of you, really. Somewhat misogynistic, too. Shame. Margie would have words to say to you about that, I imagine, if she knew what any of those terms were. But there's a silly sort of ignorance that comes with vast study of one place.

Margie twisted onto her 'back' to gaze up at her high-altitude sisters who would never know the brush of the grasses along their spine, or the way heather can tickle your skull, or how to imagine yourself wrapped around the shape of bones.

No, bones are something her sky sisters know nothing of. Bones don't take up airspace, obviously. They're held to the ground, just as Margie is. Given only the brief moment of flight before gravity has its way.

Wow, Marge. Grim.

But just this week ('week' used loosely here, of course; Margie has no sense of the King from Babylon's idea to split life into sections of sunsets) she stumbled across a new set of animal remains, bleached white by their exposure to the elements after the creature who had held them breathed for the final time.

Breath is a strange concept to the mist. It's a leashing and unleashing of air within the confines of the living, a constant exchange with the world outside a body. But, eventually, a body stops taking in the air's gift. Margie might wonder, if she could of course, whether the air feels sad when this happens. Does the air hold out extended arms for a few extra moments, scarcely believing this is really the last time it will journey through the caverns and capillaries of another? When the moments stretch, does the air let its arms drop to its side? Does it hang its head? Does it feel heavier, not to lose the piece of itself it was so ready to give?

Margie doesn't know. But perhaps she wonders.

Let's return briefly to your ageist, misogynistic idea of the eternal (again, shame). By now you have probably realized Margie does not fit into your idea of the eternal at all. Margie, whose wonder will always give her a childlike quality, whose study of place has never given her a feeling of ownership over it. No, she does not fit within your box.

How could she?

She's the mist.

Now, because Margie is a being as old as the soil being tilled across the hills and o'er the lochs, we're going to jump forward a little, in our tale. For, while there was a time that Margie lived peacefully in a solitary glen, tending only to the mushrooms blooming on what she didn't know were garden-variety logs, this was not the bulk of Margie's existence. For as long as there were rocks and falls and the echo of wingbeats, so too were the people of the Highlands. And though you may imagine it to be an uninhabited land of natural wonders, dotted with the occasional sheep (far more than occasional, those fuzzy, ghostly bastards), Margie did not know the land as such. It was not always as quiet as can be. Once, in fact, just as Margie heeded the call of her sister waters, so too did she follow the cry of a child of the glen.

But what might the mist call her own?

Certainly not the children of man.

And what might children call their own?

Certainly not the land they first walked.

Margie and the Headless Pine

On another day just like any other, Margie floated down the rocky crags of a mountain edge. Floated because she still didn't have a body, and the rocky crags because – never mind, you get it. Although she always has existed and always will, Margie remains confined to one small glen in the land we call Scotland. She doesn't call it this, of course; she's known and dwelt within this place long before there were people to name things. Being as she is a somewhat sentient miracle of nature - a suspension of water droplets, drawn and driven by the change in temperature and humidity on a small island on the small blue dot some humans named Earth - Margie doesn't think of such grand things as space and time, of universes or distant oceans. Why would she? All she needs and all she could want is in this glen on the Isle of Mist.

With that established, on this day she felt quite content, settling down from the height of the mountain on one edge of her glen. This side of the mountain face was rocky and bare, and she enjoyed softening it with her waters, watching the tendrils run, and the rocks glisten. If you were on the mountain face that day, you might have looked around for the origin of the sound of wingbeats.

But you are not on the mountain face. No one is.

For in this glen, no man had yet settled. Of course, humans did pass through in the Neolithic years that brought the two-legged creatures to this isle, and in those wandering years since. But none decided to settle here, in this glen squeezed between two mountains, constantly misty and forested. And Margie didn't mind, for the sounds of the forest with its deer and crossbills were a welcome enough soundtrack for her wonderings. The pulse of the mycelium and the rush of the water a perfect backdrop for her admiration.

She had long been a caretaker of this space and liked to think it appreciated her presence, that the heather waved as she floated by, and the deer's nose crinkled bashfully beneath her passing kisses.

Margie decided today was as good a day as any other to check on the movement of the pines across the land. She appreciated the way they raised their children, letting them spread their boughs further from the shade of their mothers. As such, the reach of the forest stretched and moved its way across her glen. Margie twisted towards the newest stretch of glade and dove between the trunks, wetting them with the bits of herself she was willing to leave behind.

She could hear the roots mingle far below the surface, and knew they were communicating with each other as they passed along vital nutrients. She floated over the bodies of the fallen trees, and under downturned arms reaching for the ones they'd lost. When some succumb to disease or the bolts of fire from the skies, their bodies are broken down to feed the rest of their growing family. Such is the way of the forest. It seemed a good system to her.

When you have existed and will exist for as long as Margie, birth and its consequential death is no large thing to be feared or grieved. It is not a callousness, per say, but simply the pragmatism that comes from such a long-lived perspective. Each mushroom, while individually wondrous, is just another piece of its mother body, offered to the land above the soil. When devoured, it goes on to nourish the forest and may again propagate more life when its remains are spread. And though each tree has its own ring record of life lived, when it falls to the ground its strength is taken back into the loam where the next tree to grow will bear a piece of its long-dissolved image. There's a beauty, to Margie, in the eternity of this place, where each leaf and moth and fungus is just a glittering sparkle in time, like the fleeting sun spots on the ever-rolling stream.

When the wind howled through to prune the branches, she trusted the other elements of nature to care for their shared home. And when Margie floated over the gnarled old log, she caressed it in thanks for its offering that allows the little ones to continue their spread.

But on this day, when Margie lifted herself up between the branches, an unfamiliar crash was heard among the boughs. The echo reverberated between twigs and sprigs — the trees quaked low in the earth. She was not entirely fluent in the language the trees spoke with one another in silences, but the feeling was a hum in the soil and in the spaces between the branches. A flock of birds took flight across the glade, and their wingbeats were not the sound of a mist sprite's laughter. No, something deeply wrong had sent them to find comfort in the waters of her sky sisters. As she watched them depart, Margie realized she was no longer alone in her glen. Someone else had entered, had changed it without the permission of the forest. Without consulting the soil.

Another crash came and she could see it this time, the crown of the pine that slipped, headless, to the ground.

Margie didn't know the name for the feeling pulsing through her droplets. She recalled the beat of mycelium and the vibrations of tree roots, but neither of those had a word to explain the feeling running its dreadful fingers along her misty form. This feeling was not wonder, not admiration or joy. Those she knew. Those she saw mirrored in the nature with whom she shared this glen. None knew the feeling she had now, but you might, reader. You might name it fear.

Before this day, Margie had not known fear. And though it would be long before she'd learn the name for it, she would know the feeling forevermore.

Margie and the Land Breakers

You could say that Margie blinked and one hundred years passed since the day the trees fell.

But Margie could not blink.

She had no eye lids.

So, Margie was forced to watch as the newcomers came and settled in her glen. They cut down trees to build a canopy about their heads. (Why they couldn't use the cover of the living ones, she didn't understand. They preferred the dried-out carcasses, it seemed.) They also exhumed rocks from the earth, stacked them high, and made borders to block out the wind and herself.

This process made no sense to Margie. She had not seen creatures do this before; no other being of the glen had fingers strong enough to dig into the soil and lift boulders. The bears had no tools with which to crack the granite, and it was odder still to imagine deer working together to lift the stones with a grunt. Once the rocks were stacked, the humans would brush their hands on the cloths wrapped around their frames. Margie would watch the movement with curiosity as their hands rested on their hips while dust and soil fell back to the earth. It seemed these creatures were not naturally equipped to survive in the glen, but like the bees, perhaps, they had a system of survival. As long as they were together.

When the first tree fell only two humans had come, a man with fur on his face and a woman with long fur gathered on her scalp. Margie knew what mated pairs were, for the deer and the doves had taught her, so she recognized these two for what they were. The humans worked hard in a way that reminded her of the birds preparing their nests, and by the time winter had laid its first blanket over the land, the mates were safe within their walls. She heard the way they held each other, and she guessed they were keeping each other warm, the way the bears did.

When spring came the woman was swollen with child, and Margie found she was glad they'd made a soft nest in her glen. For though their initial arrival in her land was a concerning surprise, Margie soon learned that this mother and her mate were not intentionally cruel in their treatment. In fact, one morning as she settled down the grassy slope to watch them, she saw the man split open a tree cone and bury it in the soil, something time took much longer to do. She marveled at the way they could use their fingers in the bringing forth of new life for the land.

After many days passed, the air growing warm while the mother grew heavy with young, her mate fashioned a tool of stone and wood. Margie watched as he raised it above the land and allowed gravity's pull to crack the soil. She flinched. But then the mates labored beside each other, using their fingers to plant new life into the soil again and again. She didn't know the word for this concept of speeding along and guiding nature's propagation, but, as the sprouts came up, she found she liked it. When the heat of the sun threatened to dry out the little plot of land, she gladly settled over the tender leaves, shielding them with her moisture. This seemed to make the humans happy, so Margie continued.

When the first cool breeze blew through and Margie's mist turned to frozen fractals on the grass, the man and woman put their plot to sleep. All the food they'd grown was tucked safely between their stone walls and below their wooden canopy. While the winds howled and the humans remained burrowed, Margie felt a new feeling she didn't know the name for. She wanted to ask the humans their name for the feeling, but she had no lips with which to form her question. This only added to her discomfort. What do you call the longing of the mist for something out of reach?

Remember, reader, when fear first introduced itself to Margie's growing understanding of emotion? For some time that feeling had been replaced by familiar curiosity, wonder, and admiration. Then there was this new undefined emotion, which you might call longing. But, one night in early winter, fear reared its sinewy head again, like the adders that slithered under the rocks in the upper forest.

The fear slinked through Margie's particles at the sound of a piercing cry. The woman's vocal cords were screaming new words into the air. But the holes they called windows were covered and the door, though unlocked, was latched closed. As you might know, the mist cannot lift a latch. And so, while the mother screamed into the dark of night, her panting breaths leaking through the small cracks between stones, Margie waited. You might, if you had been in the glen that night, have thought the mist's movement strange, almost pacing before the entrance of the small cottage by the stream.

When the screaming stopped, Margie wondered if air could hold its own breath because that is what it seemed to do. Even the trees, thankful for the continued propagating of their children, leaned in to listen. To wait.

A small, weak cry rose to the twinkling stars and the first flakes of snow.

Margie's fear shifted; babes were not supposed to be born alongside the white of winter. Did these creatures not know? Was their nest warm enough? Margie thought to ask the birds and the deer and the beavers in the waters, and she wrang herself dry with fretting for the small one kept from her by stones too cold, stones made cooler by her own moisture. She resolved then to stay atop the mountain and within the trunks of the glade if it would keep her coolness from seeping its greedy hands into the lungs of one too young to fight it.

The days passed. Evenings and mornings, sunrises and sunsets. The nights continued to grow darker and longer, but then the days reclaimed their time. And all the while Margie waited, burrowed low to the loam, a layer of frost you might attribute to the altitude. She watched the smoke rise from the hole in their grassy roof, for she could not close her eyes (no eyelids, remember?). She watched as the man occasionally emerged to get more of the cut tree they'd prepared for the flames. She tried to read him, the way she'd read the grass or the waters, for any sign of what was to come. Eventually she resigned herself to unknowing, for five hundred sun visits were not nearly long enough to have an intimate knowledge of these new creatures. Instead, she laid low among the brown hibernating heather, wishing (and not wishing) that she could sleep like the bears to wake when it was over. When she'd been still for too long, the deer occasionally checked on her, their wiggling noses kissed by her frost.

The birds returned and began to sing again. Margie let herself lift from the ground, thawing with the sun's break through her sky sisters above. If she had joints, they would be stiff and crackly with the shedding of winter's stillness. If she could, she'd stretch and shed the dust that had settled in her particles. She wished for a moment she had hands, and clothes on which to dust them off.

When Margie heard a new song, she was pierced by a new feeling, one she let seep into her watery memory. With a whirl that licked up the last of her frost into the warming breath of the earth, Margie found the little one wrapped tightly in its mother's arms. The song was the mother's creation as she introduced the babe to the warming sun. Margie found another weakness of her form — no vocal cords of her own to vibrate.

The mother wandered the land, bouncing in a new way, from one hip to the other. All the while the child blinked against the brightness that welcomed her. Margie wove and dipped beneath the pine branches once more, staying at a distance lest she still be too chilled for the fragile one. But now she was glad she had no eyelids, for it seemed one blink might make this little creature grow too fast.

Margie and the Songs

Margie had known the miracle of motherhood in her eons of existence in the glen. Of course, of course she knew the care and tenderness of a mother for her young. The way the mother deer would lead the danger away from her fawns and teach them how to be still in the watching. The way the mother birds would feed their young and teach them how to soar at the sounds of laughter.

But there was a difference in the mothering ways of the humans.

From that first day when the first woman emerged with her first young, Margie marveled at how the women changed. They entered the glade women but emerged from the screaming nights with a determination, a resilience, a ferocity. They bounced their young on their hips, they wrapped them closely to their chests. But Margie's favorite change was in their song. The mother birds sang, of course they did. But the human mothers' songs changed when they held their young. Margie, keeping back whenever she feared her mist would frost the young too soon, would 'crane her neck' to listen as the melody rose to the boughs that quivered, as it echoed off the stony slopes and melted into the stream.

Because while she was initially afraid of the impact of their presence in the land, she soon felt these creatures were home here. They welcomed the land, cared for it, and so she felt the land cared for them, too. It opened before their farming fingers, and gave them the fruit of its soil. (She learned the human term 'farming' after that first little plot grew and more humans came to help with the planting and pulling.) Margie trusted the land. She trusted the mountains and the grasses, the heather and the stones. If they welcomed these new ones into her glen, then so would she.

And it was easy to see why the earth cradled them. Their laughter was like the brook, their song like the birds. The little ones, when grown enough to walk, would skip and jump like the fawns, would pounce like the foxes, and shriek with joy like the sparrows as they played in the puddles her sky sisters made.

Margie liked the little ones best.

When they flattened themselves to the earth to watch a cricket hop, or tried to stand still so a deer wouldn't run off, Margie wondered if these traits were inherited from herself. She wondered if her own curiosity and tender wonder, her own awe and joy (joy you might call 'childlike') had permeated the air for so long that the children whose watery lungs first filled in this glen would carry forever a piece of her.

From afar she watched the children grow and age. In time, they either built their own small cottages and birthed their own wee bairns, or they moved over the hill to do so somewhere else. And this was okay. Margie, in her eons, did not flinch at change. For if you've lived as long as she has, change becomes a constant, like the tides or the seasons or the waning moon. Change can be counted on, and there was no reason for her to feel sad about it if everything that left eventually returned in a new form.

Why grieve a new moon when it will be full again? Why grieve barren branches when they will flower soon enough? Why fear times of drought when the streams will again flood their edges? So, Margie did not grieve when the young ones left; more would come.

At first, she thought the same of death. It was just as the mushrooms grew and unfurled just to fade, just as the young leaves greened only to color and fall back to the earth. More mushrooms would come. More leaves would green.

But humans did not think the same of death. They did not 'shrug their shoulders' (something Margie often wished she could physically do, and perhaps practiced when she was far enough up the forest for only the adders to mock her). They did not just wait for the new life to come.

No, they had new sounds for death.

New songs.

When the first woman passed, when she stopped taking the air's offered gift, a great wail rose from her children gathered around. Margie had never known a grief so loud it could shake the stone, but she thought this one might.

Then the glen children made a new garden. They dug again into the soil, and broke the stones in new ways. They planted the woman's body into the earth, and Margie, for longer than she'd like to admit, wondered if they had learned to farm themselves the way they farmed the food. For many nights Margie watched the new stone garden for a sprout, a tender shoot. None came, and Margie wondered if the humans were sad for this failed crop.

Perhaps it needed more moisture. Perhaps, like in that first summer, the young plants needed her mist. Perhaps this gift would bring them joy.

So, Margie drew near. She swam through the air, low and fast, then slow and steady. She filled the stone garden and settled down to it. There were dried and dying pale yellow flowers, now nearly white, cut by the woman's offspring and laid across the ground and stone. Lazy planting, Margie thought. She knew this mother had taught her children better; this was not the fastest way to propagate.

But Margie had watched the mother and her mate. *She* had learned. Margie laid her misty 'hands' to the disturbed dirt still not overcome by the moss and heather. She had no fingers, no ability to make impressions, no strength with which to dig. But water does.

Margie pulled her droplets together and let them create rivulets, burying the flowers under the ground, hoping the pressure would open the seeds for her.

Of course, this one night of grave watering did not produce fruit. The planted dead did not sprout, not yet. She had learned that farming took time.

For many months Margie came and laid her mist upon the mother, resting softly atop the soil under which she laid.

But when a meager harvest came across the fields, when the humans worked in sullen silence together to gather what food they could, Margie didn't know the name for the feeling she felt at that dirt plot left unharvested.

Margie accepted that this crop had failed. That winter, she stayed atop the heights, away from the new bairns she'd meet in spring. This too, was a rhythm Margie learned to trust.

Of course, as all patterns do, this occasionally diverged.

That winter, three small stones joined the first large one. When they planted the young ones, Margie wondered how the mountain didn't crack with the sounds of their grief, with the new songs they screamed into cold skies who cared nothing for the comings and goings of those kept to the earth.

The first warm kisses of spring brought new greening leaves. Green, but still tightly curled. Margie recognized the feeling. For the memory of what was lost kept her curled in around the hole, unsure if she was ready to unfurl into the new season of comings and inevitable goings.

What unfurled her was a new sound. It was a faint one, one she only heard because of the way the breath mixed with the still cool air of early spring.

A wordless gasp.

A sound of wonder.

Margie followed the vibrations, ever curious, hoping she might yet find the young who made it through another winter.

Instead, she found one young woman, not yet a mother, no longer a child. By the basket over her arm, Margie assumed she'd been sent out to see what she could gather, to see if the earth was yet ready to start its nourishing.

What the woman found in the stone garden was not the harvest Margie had long hoped for. It was not a harvest that would fill their bellies or sate their thirst. But by the brightness in the woman's eyes, Margie would have thought the earth had offered up the grandest feast.

For throughout the stone garden, flowers had bloomed.

New water fell from the woman's eyes. The air became salty when the other humans came to witness the truth of her excited news. Margie had seen loss pour rain down the landscape of their faces, but this water tasted different. It came with smiles and embraces, wiggled noses of new mothers upon the noses of their new young.

She was glad her small gift had not been missed, had not been misplaced. She found she was glad to have more time to study these humans whose songs had stormed the mountains, and had, for one night, allowed the mist to be a farmer.

Margie and the Burning Ones

For the next many days (hundreds upon hundreds of them, in fact), Margie continued her study of the humans as their roots dug deeper into Highland landscape. The young grew and the ground changed under their feet ('feet' used literally, this time, for as you know, humans do, in fact, have feet).

Just as the deer carve and keep to their faithful paths, so too did the humans create their own avenues through the glen. Their favorite treks flattened under the quickened steps of children running to and fro, from one cottage to the next. Some paths were worn more quickly than others, while some were eventually overgrown.

After enough years, these paths seemed the best and only way to walk. They continued to tread them until no one remembered who started them, or why they wound the way they did. The ground grew up around the paths, and the dense, hardy grasses hung off the earthen walls that bordered them, giving the elders something to lean against while the quicker ones passed. Margie found she cherished it, cherished it better because she remembered every person who started the paths, every one who cleared an ankle-turning stone, and all those who had stubbed a toe on it in the years before.

The decades and centuries (as we know to call them) took their time changing Margie too, like the ocean tides against the cliffs of this very isle (which she had never seen). While she initially stayed back from the humans, only occasionally leaning in to shield the young plants or water the dead, now she crept closer, even as far as kissing their thatched roofs in the winter when she felt their absence most keenly.

Spring remained her favorite for the meeting of new bairns, the reemergence of the families, the cheeriness of their labor as they set to seeding the earth for the coming year. There was something about those first days of warm sun that, while not erasing the losses of the darkened winter, made Margie thankful for their resilience, their tenacity. She marveled when the women gathered around tables with new wool and odorous waste, somehow making music from it, somehow raising rhythms that changed the very fabrics in their hands.

Margie continually wondered at the way humans were when they existed in groups, in communities. A honeybee only has one sting, but she had once seen a swarm from the hive bring down a boar. So too were these humans a powerful force when gathered. They could change a glen — could change the very mist itself.

Her study of the humans consumed her and eventually Margie began to notice differences between each person. One would laugh through their nose, while another laughed with their whole body. One child would cry at a loud bird caw, while another could be losing red water from a wound without noticing. One mother would sing to her child while bouncing, and another would sway instead. Margie began to study each person the way she'd studied the individual mushrooms; she found she cherished them the same way. Individually marvelous, for as long as she had them.

As they wormed their way deeper into her admiration, she soon felt she didn't have them for long enough. With each new addition to the stone garden, Margie felt a weight to her moisture. She still didn't know the word for missing or longing, but it's what she felt when the flowers overgrew the graves each spring. When the loss was too keen, the people marveled at the thick frost in the graveyard, and how even the sun didn't seem to melt it.

She still hated the small stones most.

She would always hate the small stones most.

It seemed these passings came in waves; some winters had greedy hands that claimed too many, added too many small stones to the corner yard.

One year, when the borders of the stone garden expanded its prior limit, Margie felt a shift. Suddenly, it seemed too hard to lean in, to watch the individual differences, to find herself admiring each individual child like her favorite mushrooms only to lose them to sickness, harm, or poor harvests. For once, Margie disliked her curious heart, her inclination to marvel and treasure. That spring she didn't revel in the unfurling green. No, she found she started to resent it, for it meant a coming frost. An inevitable death.

For what could Margie do against illness and injury? She already protected the crops and kept them watered, but when the soil refused to yield, what power has the mist to fill young bellies, to keep the weakness from their bones? Perhaps it was best she withdraw, pull back up to the mountain top where the stones don't mark another loss, nor it's choking grasp.

That year, the humans may have wondered at the warmth, at the absence of the cooling mist, and why it stayed atop the mountain to watch them toil.

She didn't like feeling like her sky sisters, removed from the ache of bones, distant from the cries of children with skinned knees.

She heard those cries, still. Of course, of course she did. Have you ever been to a glen in the Highlands? The sounds rise and fall, echoed and mimicked by every rocky curve and hollow. While Margie wished she had eyelids to close, she wished even more to have hands with which to cover ears. She'd seen the one they call Mara do this when she was young and the sounds of toil grew too loud. Of course, this meant Margie would also need ears, something else she didn't have. No, all she could do was absorb the sound waves of the cries when Bruce (Mara's young one) tripped on that not-yet-removed stone on that one not-yet-fully-smoothed path.

Margie had to admit then that she was glad the humans had learned the land's gentle remedies. For when Mara lifted Bruce, smoothed his hair from his damp face, and planted soothing kisses on his brow, Margie trusted that Mara knew how to treat the wound. Margie trusted her like she trusted the wind in its tree pruning and trusted the dry stream to fill again. Mara had long ago learned of the one weed in the Old Wood that, when ground up, would stop the bleeding of a skinned knee. She knew of the other root that, when stuck in water over a fire, would stop the spread of infection.

For though these humans were not equipped on their own for natural survival, the land seemed to provide, seemed to want to keep them around. While the men were listening to the distant rumblings of coming storms, the women listened to the plants and the earth. Margie trusted Mara to tend to the child's injury, just as she trusted her to prepare treatment for the too-young mother, or the elderly man's painful joints. Margie was glad that, although she could not bring herself to lean in, there remained other curious spirits who could provide the care the mist could not.

In this relaxed trust, and relative distance, Margie did not notice the hushed voices and spread whispers. Margie did not catch the quick glances and slight shuffles.

But she did taste the change in the air.

That night in the glen, Margie shifted at the dots of torches crossing the hill and descending into the valley. She pulled up and leaned off the mountain's stony spires, hovering for a moment in the watching. They drew closer, further in. Margie knew there were more humans over the hill now, knew because the family who filled her glen would occasionally disappear and return with more supplies. It seemed the world had shifted beyond these valley walls, just as the land had bent and Margie had changed.

Thus, initially, when the crowd descended like a flock to the little cottages that sprouted up to hold her family, Margie thought perhaps they had planned a gathering. They had done this occasionally. Usually she'd know of it, but usually she'd be down in the valley. She just missed the news, that's all.

But that wasn't all.

Margie knew it when a scream rent the air.

Before Margie could stop her curious heart, she was floating down the mountain edge, pulled by a voice she knew, a cry she'd known since the girl was young, long before the girl was a mother who knew how to treat skinned knees and painful joints.

Margie descended faster as more shouts joined Mara's screaming. She floated between cottages and over thatched roofs until she saw it, the crowd of humans she didn't know, swarming like angry bees. In the middle was Mara. Mara with ropes around her arms and feet, kneeling before the small loch at the base of the stream. One man had a book raised above his head and he was saying words Margie did not know. The words had the crowd nodding, had the crowd making motions over their heads and chests, had them spitting on the ground in front of Mara's kneeling, shaking form.

Margie didn't know what words could turn her humans into hornets. Not all of them, of course. Mara's mate was raging, screaming, held at bay by stronger arms. Margie didn't need to know the words to know the feeling. It sliced through her when his final yell tore through the glen, punctuated by a splash, and then silence. Held breath. Bubbling waters. Bubbles slowing.

Margie didn't know why the humans planted Mara in the water. But she didn't like it. She didn't know why they exhumed her later, still as stone, only to let the flames devour breathless body.

Margie did not understand. And honestly, reader, no amount of explanation would have made her. No comprehension of words from book or tongue could have convinced her that this daughter of the glen, and many others like her across the hills and hollows, should have been so cruelly removed from the living.

Given not even a stone in the corner yard to mark their absence.

But Margie marked their absence.

Margie marked it in every root she knew would have stopped the infection which claimed more young ones that year because Mara wasn't there to help.

Margie marked her absence in the bubbling brook which reminded her of that one horrible silence after screams rent the unbothered skies.

Margie created a space within her droplets for Mara's memory, more permanent than any stone in the graveyard.

Margie felt a new feeling in those weeks and months after the smoke ebbed and the burning ones were taken from her. Stolen from their glen.

The mist learned how to be angry.

And Margie was forever changed.

Margie and the Broken Tongues

Margie was not alone in her anger. In fact, over the next decades it seemed everyone was angry. Unfortunately, they were not all angry about the women stolen from the land to spend their last breaths in the lochs and still pools. Margie wondered if even the air was angry that it had its final goodbye stolen. Maybe that was what caused the shift in the breeze.

For every air taker was plunged into a new restlessness and anxiety. In the past, Margie's humans heard murmurs and sometimes spread them, but here in this glen, they were somewhat deaf to the changes occurring across the isle. And, of course, Margie couldn't warn them; she had no way of knowing. No, while the humans disappeared over the rises to return with new burdens (visible and invisible), Margie stayed. This was Margie's home, her glen. The pocket of land she had cared for longer than there were words for the feeling.

Speaking of words for feelings, Margie, as you have probably noticed, has picked up quite a few by now. She's learned about fear, then longing, sadness, and now anger. These feelings began to rattle through her on a regular basis now, now that the men were taken from their cottages for more days than Margie liked to count. And, when they returned, there were always less. Sometimes they brought the bodies to be planted in the stone garden. Sometimes they didn't. She wasn't sure which was sadder.

New men in red cloths appeared. They hadn't moved into her glen, but Margie thought they must have set up a cottage just on the other side of the rise, for how often they visited. She learned quickly that she did not like these visitors. She did not like how they treated her humans, her family. In fact, on some nights when the air was particularly cool, Margie would flatten herself to the perpetually muddy road leading up the rise and let her moisture ice it over. When they came over it the morning they would trip or slide. Margie liked that quite a lot.

She had to stop, though; for when the ones in the red felt anger, they were mean about it, sometimes so cruel in their toppling of carts and stomping of gardens that Margie felt her mist warm for the anger in her.

Sometimes they didn't stop at harming the carts and gardens. Sometimes it was her women, her men, her children that they harmed. Margie felt at fault for this. Would we call that guilt? Perhaps. Perhaps she did feel guilty for tripping the men who took it out on her humans. Was it Margie's fault? Of course not. But Margie had yet to be exposed to people who believed they had ownership of land and humans who were not theirs. So far, her humans had treated the land and each other, for the most part, with respect and care.

These men in the red cloths did not.

It only added to Margie's anger. Anger she did not know

where to put. Does it fit next to the memory of those taken from her? Or should it go beside the feeling of fear that blossomed each time she fell in love with a new human? Where does anger fit, when she has too much else to hold?

Margie didn't know.

It seemed her humans didn't either.

For one night in early spring, when the coolness allowed Margie to come right up to the cottages, she heard them talking. Talk of an uprising, whatever that meant, and of a man named something — Stuart, was it? Margie had learned many words but still had an awful time of it when she was listening through cracks of mossed-over, centuries-old stone.

She learned that, somewhere over the walls of her glen, there was one man who wanted to tell everyone what to do. Not like a father, it seemed. They called him *king*. They'd had many different ones (and one woman, though they didn't like to talk of her) over the years the humans were here. But they didn't like this one much at all. It seemed he was the one who sent the men in red; Margie resolved that she didn't like him either.

She didn't know what the men thought they would do about this king over the hills, but apparently it meant getting together in groups and moving about with new sticks, shouting while banging against stone and metal. At first it was small groups, gathering quietly in the evenings when the ones in red didn't usually come. Slowly, more and more came over the rises with their sticks and shouts. It seemed this made the men feel better, gave them a place to put their anger. Margie thought perhaps she should try it, but no matter how many times she tried to form fingers from her mist, they were never strong enough to lift the swords or spears she found stuffed behind the barn.

Still, she tried. The men thought it odd that their weapons were damp in the mornings.

Then, faster than they had gathered together with their sticks and shouts, they were all gone. Leaving only silence in their wake.

Margie found she missed the pangs and glints of metal. She found she missed the way they patted each other on the back and made each other laugh with their whole chests. She had missed that in these last many days, and it was good to see the men smile again. Margie hoped they would get what they wanted, and that when they came home their cheer would come with them.

But they didn't come home.

Margie watched as the women shifted. She watched as they tried to keep calm spirits in front of the children, only to share glances with one another when the young ones weren't looking. Margie watched as nerves turned to concern, and then to deep fear. She watched as they slept less at night, watched as each passing songbird and spug made them look to the glen walls, to the entrance that should be carrying their men back to warm hearths and safe cottages.

Still, the men did not come.

Until, one day, they did.

Just not the men they wanted.

These were not Margie's men. Not the fathers and sons, brothers and uncles, husbands and cousins and the one friend they'd taken in when he had no other family to go home to.

No, those were not the men who entered the glen that day in

late April, in the year we know as 1746.

It was the men in red who came, more red on their fingers, in their carts, under their boots. It was the men in red who burned the cottages of the men who helped with the sticks and shouting. They burned every tool that could be a weapon, and every striped fabric with which her humans had clothed themselves. It was the men in red whose words rang through her glen, collapsing the women in wails Margie had thought reserved for the dead.

And death this was.

The women and children were forever changed.

The clothes they wore, the way they spoke.

You'd think their very tongues had been cut out, butchered, for the new manner of speaking that followed felt so strange in her glen, so at odds with the sounds of the brook and the birds and the howling wind.

Though Margie felt anger and fear and, yes, sadness and longing too, a far more dangerous feeling was taking root into her droplets. Her feeling was seen reflected in the sag of every shoulder, the depth of every sigh. It was the humans' tenacity and determination that first won Margie's admiration. But now it seemed all the humans and the mist could do was watch as the very air was stripped of the sounds of their people. The birds, and the air with outstretched arms, wondered why there was so much less breath to be taken, so much less song to be sung.

Margie and the Ones Who Stayed

It was amidst the thickness of this sullen air that a new wave
of children were born; more mothers made, new songs sung. The
world had turned flat and cold, and only one form of tongue was
safe with outsiders nearby. Soon the mothers' old songs that went
like:

Bà bà bà mo leanabh

Bà mo leanabh bà

Bà hù hò mo leanabh

Chan eil thu ach bà

Became,

Bring back, bring back,

Oh, bring back my Bonnie to me, to me.

Bring back, bring back,

Oh, bring back my Bonnie to me.

Unless they were in their houses alone, in the quiet safety of
their old stone walls. Walls that kept prying ears out; walls that
also kept Margie out. It felt, in some ways, like her people were

slipping away from her.

And in those next years, many did.

The extra cottages, once built to hold the centuries-expanding family, began to empty. Slowly, groups of her humans disappeared over the hill in search of food, or work, or something Margie didn't quite understand. This glen was always what she needed, and for hundreds and thousands of waxing moons it had been enough for the humans, too. But now, as smoke billowed prouder from the south and the ground could no longer be relied upon to bear food, it changed. Her glen was not enough, not for all of them.

Margie was not enough, not for all of them.

For what could the mist do to heal broken land or butchered tongues? What could the mist do against shattered spirits and the stone garden missing its sons? If Margie could, she would reshape the pass to keep them all safe within the mountains' walls, to keep the threats blocked out. If Margie could, she'd cross the hills and hollows in search of the bodies that belonged planted in her grove. If she could, she'd go back in time and prevent their training and their leaving; perhaps if she'd frosted over the sticks some more, or been strong enough to lift them and carry them away.

But, of course, she could do none of these things.

She was just the mist.

So, slowly, her glen began to clear. Just a couple of people here and there. First, a young mother who found a new mate to protect the dead one's bairn. Then boy who had been too young to have died on the far field but was now old enough to forge a new life from the wreckage. On and on the people traveled up the worn and dusty path, past the hill, out of the glen. Out of reach.

And then, finally, on a day just like any other (mind you, the kind Margie was starting to greatly dislike) she found there was just one cottage left with smoke in the chimney stack. Just one, of the once-filled family estate. This last warmed cottage had been the first, the one with the first stones exhumed from the ground, the ones whose roof was still held up by the strong trees she'd first watched fall.

Margie remembered it all. She remembered the man and woman who toiled to set up their walls before winter, who emerged with the first spring bairn, who taught Margie the words for fingers and farming. She remembered how that woman was the first planted in the corner lot, the quiet beginning of the now expansive stone garden.

And then her daughter became a mother.

And her daughter.

And hers.

And so on. Margie had watched the family tree spread and burrow its roots into her glen, becoming as much a part of the land as the stones and the soil.

Reader, if you are counting, or if (because you probably do know of the Babylonian king's decree to split life into series of seven sunsets) you're curious, Margie has lived alongside this one family for 25,498 weeks next Tuesday. That's 489 years, if you don't want to do the math; which means that this just-like-any-other day is in the year of someone's Lord 1808.

And on this just-like-any-other day, while Margie was alone with one remaining mate and mother (who was heavy with her first child, still safe en-womb), Margie was feeling things she didn't have words for.

As a human, you know the words for feelings, I presume, so

I'll tell you. She was feeling tired. She was feeling lonely. She was feeling helpless.

And worst of all, she was feeling restless. Maybe even bored.

Yes, bored. At least, much in need of a distraction. Boredom and restlessness are dangerous things for an age-old being. (Is 'being' the right word? Probably, at this point.) And in that moment, laid on her 'back' among the brambles, while the heather scratched her 'spine' and her sky sisters floated by without a care, Margie decided it was time to pay her old log a visit.

Now, this was absolutely not the same garden-variety log from the Old Wood at the beginning of our tale. That log has long since dissolved into the ground to feed the snails and miscellany mycelium that had already begun to lay claim to it those many, many moons ago, when the glen was almost as quiet as it is now.

No, the log Margie was heading for was not a garden-variety log (she knows what a garden is now, and she'd be quite proud of the fact, too — if she knew that feeling yet). This was one of the father trees, one of the first that had populated this glen when Margie was still newly assigned to the world, still learning how to think and move and be misty. This tree had been the tallest for quite some time now and, of course, as all tall and good things do, it fell with a thunderous crash. An expert might claim termites or root-rot or something. Margie, an expert in her own right on many such things, would normally have been able to tell you herself, but she'd been preoccupied with the goings on of the humans down in the glen. So, when the tree fell (and they all heard it, being in the glen when it did so) she felt a bit of sadness and a bit of guilt for not having known it was dying, not having seen the signs of the coming fall. In her restlessness she decided to check on it, to pay her respects.

Might as well.

There is no stone garden in nature, not like humans have. There would be no use in planting this corpse anyway, seeing as being planted before did not prevent its death. And besides, the mushrooms would eventually break it down and reclaim it, absorb it back into the soil for more little trees to pop up in its place. The way of nature, as it was centuries ago and as it still was on this day in the forest.

Still, the human tradition of visiting the dead had seeped into Margie, and she occasionally felt the overwhelming need to lay her mist upon their resting place, to imagine for one moment that she did not have to say goodbye.

"Hello, old friend," she would have said, if she had the mouth to say it. Again, the birds picked up the sentiment and her droplets plopped in tune. A natural sound, an everyday forest sound. She'd gladly accept the compliment on another day, when she wasn't so full of feelings, some named, others not. Just a foreboding presence, those feelings, unmarked like the graves that hold some of her glen-sons over the hills and far too far away from her.

Margie wished then that she'd spent more time with the trees, more time learning their underground language, their wisdom. She suspected they must feel a similar grief when their young are cut for structure or fire. When one is too overshadowed to grow and meets an early death. Do the trees have songs for grief, do they have funeral dirges? Would this one have known what to say to her sadness, if she'd had the ability to listen? If she'd let the years teach her the talk of the trees?

Instead, her mist gathered along the greying bark as she planted a kiss to the last of the old ones, the only one who might remember a young mist sprite who didn't know how to cry, and didn't wish she had the ability.

The sun had already begun its descent when Margie was weaving through the forest once more, heading for the edge where she could watch the humans put the land to sleep. The man had been heading out for supplies this morning, so he should be returning soon. The mother should be bringing in the clothes dried by the sun. Margie enjoyed watching their simple routines. In a time of so much change and loss, this one thing still reflected the rhythms of nature and the centuries before. This one thing gave Margie comfort.

Or, it would have.

Before the scream.

Margie and the Leanabh a' Cheo

This was not a normal scream.

It was a sound Margie had heard only a handful of times over the centuries. She had not understood it at first, why some mothers screamed differently than others. After so many generations the similarities blur and the exceptions stand out.

This scream was one of the exceptions. When mothers were this loud, often the babes were born silent. It had happened a few times. Of course, of course it had. Margie had not seen what caused the silent children as all of their births had occurred within the walls, away from the arms of the mist. But this was different. This was louder. Closer. Margie pushed herself faster until she made it through the tree line.

The mother was not in the cottage behind the walls. No, this mother was on the ground, halfway up the hill that led to the Old Wood. Her knees were in the soil, one hand gripping the heather and one wrapped around herself, holding tightly where her child had grown. A toppled basket and scattered berries and mushrooms told Margie she had been returning from the forest when she was crippled by the pain, by the pangs of her body evicting the child from her womb. But was it time?

What was wrong? And where was her mate?

Where was her mate?

Margie spread her mist wide and thin, filling the glen with a haze of glistening air as she looked and looked for him. He must not be back from over the hill. And this was wrong, this was very wrong.

Since the first birth in this glen no mother had crossed this transition alone. They had all had their mates or their mothers or other mothers with them. They were never alone, never up on the hill outside. It was not supposed to be like this.

Margie pulled her moisture together and pushed herself back through the evening air to the woman, to the mother still panting, still holding her abdomen as if she might be able to keep the child within.

When the woman screamed again, sweat glistened at her brow. Margie leaned in, leaned close. If the woman had been in less pain, perhaps she would have been startled by the sudden movement of the mist. But her eyes were closed against the strain, so all the woman knew was the soothing kiss of coolness across her skin. As the woman screamed against nature's greedy hands pulling the child from her womb, Margie stayed. She stayed as the mother sucked in the cool misty air. Margie learned what it was, then, to feel like the air and the breath. To be inhaled, to kiss the inside of inflamed airways, to soothe the heat within another. She found she liked it.

And so, she stayed.

She stayed until the man rounded the top of the rise to hear his mate screaming. Margie stayed as he sprinted down the hill, waded through the mist of the valley, and up the next hill. When he found her, Margie recognized the fear in his face as his hands found her cheeks, as he leaned his forehead against hers and whispered comfort into her sweat and tears. When more pain wracked his mate's body and she writhed against it, he was a stone, stalwart in an angry tide. When that tide ebbed, his mate nodded once, weakly. This must have freed him to get help, for he left again after a gentle caress to her cheek. Alone again, the woman screamed into the darkness of the fallen night.

And Margie stayed.

Margie stayed until the man returned, another woman in tow, a woman Margie had seen use her hands in the bringing forth of human life. Gardener? No, that's not their word for it. They found the mother in the darkened mist, following the sounds of her screams. The birth woman looked her over, felt her stomach and her head. Finally she asked the man to help move the laboring one into the cottage. At this Margie felt a stirring in herself, and it tasted a bit like fear. Fear mixed with longing. She didn't want the woman pulled away, carried behind a door where she couldn't follow.

"Let her stay," Margie would have begged, if she'd the mouth to plead. The evening wind picked up her sentiments and the hooting owls translated for her, but the humans didn't know the language of the forest. The mist was powerless to ask; they were powerless to hear it. And Margie felt angry for all the things she couldn't do, couldn't have.

The mother started violently shaking her head back and forth, and Margie was the air holding its breath. The man and helper looked at the mother with concern, but when they began to object, she cut them off.

"Let me stay. Let her be a child of the mist."

Margie felt the change in herself immediately, and quickly leaned in to place more kisses to the woman's sweat. Margie had never had a child, unless you counted each individual drop left behind on the surfaces of the highlands. But she'd watched many children born, many grown, many buried. With each she met and cherished, she began to imagine herself in the skin of a mother. She had a secret wish to draw the children to herself, to pick them up and settle them on a hip, to sing one of the old natural songs and tousle their hair.

These are all things the mist cannot do. The mist has no strength of arms, no curve of hips, no voice for songs, old or new. Margie had long since resigned herself to this, to studying the children and their mothers from afar before watching them slip between her weak and misty fingers.

"Let her be *a leanabh a' cheo*," the mother said again, slipping into the old language they still used among themselves in the dark and quiet places. A child of the mist, it meant. And Margie swelled with the feeling we've named 'pride,' pulling the coolness closer to the woman's heated forehead, filling her breaths with evening kisses, willing her to know the mist accepted its role. The mist was happy to mother, in whatever way she could.

After minutes more of screaming and mist-breathing, the babe came with a gush of red water. Margie, for all of the cycles of birth and death she had witnessed, had never seen this part of a woman's labor. In the rush of blood she saw the skinned knees, the burning of flesh, the blood under foreign boots. She saw the hearth fires and warm embers and steaming soups. She saw the harvests and the toil. Margie wondered then if being a mother meant the spilling of blood, not just in the initial labor, but in all of the labor to come. In the sleepless nights and early mornings, in the sharing of milk and chapping of breasts, in the healing of skinned knees and being stolen from the world for knowing how.

For a moment the child was silent, and the humans held their breath. The air had its arms outstretched, waiting to be accepted for the first time. Margie had no time for fear; this was a child of the mist, her mist, and if she had learned anything from these generations of mothers, it was that she would be proud to be counted as one of them. So Margie poured herself around the babe, around the water in the child's lungs, willing it to breathe her in.

When the babe first cried and the water vibrated with the sound, the relief taught Margie why water always streamed down the new mothers' faces; why it now licked down this one's cheeks. Margie could not cry, so she welcomed this saltwater into herself. It tasted different than the salt of their sadness or their toil. It was the salt of deep joy, of relief, of the weary exhale after labor.

The father leaned in and planted kisses across the new mother's brow as his own tears wet his beard. The birth woman was helping with the after pangs and sent the father off for supplies. All the while, the mother gazed upon her babe, and Margie gazed upon the mother, wishing more than ever that she could be so fair, so strong, so resilient.

When the mother whispered something sweet to the child in their old tongue, the child opened her eyes to the world, to the stars barely blinking through the gathered mist. Margie memorized the color of those eyes, for she'd learned they do not always stay as they first begin. She never wanted to forget the midnight waters that first took in her misty form.

As Margie soaked it all in, made space in her particles for new goodness, the helper woman asked the mother for a name. Even now, sweat soaked and worn, humans name things.

The mother stroked her daughter's cheek, refusing to take her eyes off the reflected stars in the half-shrouded skies. "My *leanabh a' cheo*. My Aila."

Aila.

Margie had remembered every child of the glen, the sound of their footfalls and giggles, the sound of their whispered secrets and proud stances. But since the loss of Mara, Margie had not held onto their names.

She would hold onto this one.

Aila. From a resilient place.

Margie's very own daughter of the mist.

II

AILA + MARGIE

THE CHILD AND THE MIST

I blink against bright light.
Cradled here in Mama's arms, she keeps me close.
Her hand hovers, my eyes rest in the shadow.
It's not enough. The world is too bright.
I start to cry. It's all too much.
Suddenly cool, my eyelids no longer backlit red.
I slowly blink them open; the sun shrouded
by gentle grey.

Mama is smiling up, talking.
Who is she talking to?
Who granted me this shade?
Mama's eyes are back on mine and she smiles.
She tells me something,
something I wish I could understand.
Mama speaks two ways; one around others,
one with just me when we're among the trees
or by the stream.

A Mist Sprite's Study of Being Human

She sings it as she sways me to sleep.
I wish I knew what she's saying.
I wish I knew how to move my mouth like that.
I wish I knew who she talks to,
I wish I knew who to thank for this coolness,
that soothes me back to sleep.

I'm older now.
I've learned my name is Aila.
And I learned the word for Mama's friend is cheo.
When I got my mouth to form the letters
and my throat to make the sounds,
Mama cried. But she smiled while she cried,
so maybe it's okay.

Mama took me to the trees today
I sat in the dirt while she talked about the trees,
and the mushrooms she was picking,
and sang some of her favorite songs.
When the air got cool and wet Mama smiled
like she does when she sees a friend.

When the night comes, I'm warm
Tucked between Mama and Papa.
They talk and I don't understand,
but the sound of their voices
lulls me to sleep.

A Mist Sprite's Study of Being Human

Today I took my first steps.
I walked! Can you believe it?
I've been trying so hard.
Mama took me to the trees, and sat me by the log.
She went behind it and I got scared.
I pulled myself up on it and yelled for her.
I saw her. She saw me.
She crouched with arms out and called to come to her,
to be in her arms.
That is my very favorite place to be so I
stepped.

The moss was cool under my feet.
And the wind through the trees
sounded like people clapping
Like Mama clapping
so I stepped
and
stepped.

With a sound like a whoosh, a pitter, a plop
I made it to Mama. She kissed me,
and I heard birds
taking flight.

Mama let me carry the basket today.
We went up to the trees
And I carried the basket all by myself.
Mama has been sad.
I want to make her happy by carrying the basket.
There's not much else I know how to do.
She's still sad. I think it's been too dry.
There are no berries, and it's hard to find the mushrooms.
We look on the log, and then on the other.
We go further into the forest than I've gone before.
I got scared.

I held onto her skirts and squeezed.
We looked and looked.
We almost went home.
But then Mama gasped.
I thought something was wrong,
Until I saw the mist.
It came winding through the trees, past us.
Mama grabs my hand.
She says it's leading us, and so we follow.

The mist is cool and makes the woods spooky.
I watch Mama's face but
She doesn't look scared.
She looks calm, excited.
I try to be calm and excited too.
I want to look like her.

And then Mama cries, "Mushrooms!"
And the forest makes its noises,
and the birds start flying.

I squat to look at the clump of mushrooms
growing like flowers at the bottom of an oak.
Mama wipes a tear from her cheek,
And I think I hear her speak her thanks.
But the forest was so loud
with its whooshes and pitter plops
That I couldn't say for sure.

Just as the child was growing up, you might be tempted to say Margie was too. Which is silly, of course. Margie wasn't growing up. How could she be? She's as ancient as the soil and older than these trees.

But somehow, watching this little one, Margie felt herself change.

At the girl's birth, Margie accepted her role.

She'd seen it happen so many times over the years that she shouldn't have been surprised. She watched every woman change when they became a mother. Why wouldn't motherhood change the mist, too?

When Aila first looked up at the bright spring sun, Margie was there to shroud it. When Aila first spoke their name for her, Margie leaned in and planted kisses all over the girl and her mother. And when Aila took her first steps, barefoot in the forest, Margie was laughing with joy.

When the land was dry and the mushrooms sparse, Margie pulled her weakened state together to lead the pair through the deep dark trees to where the land had held onto some moisture. Margie said 'mushrooms' over and over again, as best she could. When the trees and birds translated for her with their everyday forest sounds, it seemed perhaps her dear ones understood. Maybe they were learning, just as she was. Maybe they were learning together.

Margie thought through the centuries she had spent studying these humans as they formed the land and grew alongside it. That was good, but these recent months and years had been different. Since Aila's birth, Margie let herself draw near, let them know her the way she's known them. What would have been different if she'd done this before? Would she somehow have been able to save Mara, and the many sick after her loss? Would Margie have taught them the way of the forest just like they taught her their ways? Would it have changed something? She had long felt so powerless. A brief observer of even briefer lives.

But now, with Aila and the final father and mother, Margie has a place. She has things she can do, ways she can be. They notice and thank her. They *see* her.

And she, in turn, sees them. She sees the daughter trying hard to walk on the spongey moss and finally succeeding. She sees the mother strongly shouldering her own fear while cultivating wonder for her young. She sees the father carefully tending the weak ground, burning the kelp and spreading it, coaxing the life from it to feed his family when the food grows scarce.

Margie watched, despite the losses, as the humans clawed and fought their way to carve out a life together in a place that wanted them still.

She wanted them still.

So when the girl called her name, when the mother recognized her beckon and thanked her for their harvest, or when the man smiled at her mist gently laying atop his fields, she decided this is how it always should be.

Always will be.

The people loved her land, and she loved them back.

She *loved.*

Margie could twirl up to the stars at the thought, at the feeling.

Is this what has driven her humans? Is this the thread that has woven them together, given them something to strive for besides survival and need?

She feels her droplets quiver and warm, a shiver down her 'spine.' Yes, she loved.

She loved these humans; she loved her child of the mist.

She loved.

She loved the trees in the forest, and the mushrooms growing over them.

She loved the hills and their slopes.

She loved her sister waters giggling as they fell, and she loved her sky sisters despite their ignorant indifference.

She loved how the wind whipped and howled and played with her moisture.

She loved this glen.

Now that she knows the feeling and the word for it, she sees she always has loved. This is what drove her to grieve the women planted in soil and water, and the men who screamed for them. This is what drove her to check on the logs who fell and the young who replaced them. This is what made her want to learn their language. This is what drives her again and again to the edge of the forest to watch her humans in their waking and sleeping, this is what spreads her wide and gently over their fields and farms. This is the call in her 'bones' to protect and provide and do something with her weak, misty arms.

Margie halts her spinning and twirling as a new thought comes.

Over the last thousands of sunrises, she has learned many feelings, learned to name them and hold them. Is she — she can hardly bring herself to fully think it, to allow hope to sprout up and cradle it.

Is she becoming like them?

Could she, could she be —?

She remembers how she long wrapped herself around the shape of bones, imagined what it would be like to have a form, a strength of structure and spine. She didn't have humans living in her glen then, so she imagined being a stag or a bear, a fox or even a squirrel. None of these had felt right. None fit.

But now, as Margie watches the smoke of cooking mushrooms rise from the hole in the cottage roof, she wonders if none of those were the right bones. Was she, perhaps, supposed to be human all along?

Not fully human, of course. She could never match the might and strength and gentle forbearance of those creatures. She could never master their quirks and odd endearments, like how they sneeze when the sun is too bright, or how they seem drawn to watch the sun set behind the mountains no matter how many times it happens.

No, for all of Margie's wonder and childlike joy, she knows she could not be quite fully human. But perhaps she could pretend, just for a time. Perhaps she's been slowly evolving. Perhaps she could now be at her zenith. Closest to something that will always be partly separate.

The Mist and the Garden

Mama looks beautiful in her sleep.
    The evening light is coming through the space
    under the curtain, falling across her hair,
    which is falling across her face.
    Papa is snoring like a bear,
    which often makes me laugh.
    But I am not laughing tonight.

No, the moon woke me,
    ever so rudely, shining brightly against
    the insides of my eyelids.
    Whispering into my brain like mother,
    when it's time to wake.
    But it is not time to wake,
    and I don't know why the moon
    thinks it is so.

I slip out from under the covers and twist,

My tunic brushes along the back of my calves
as I kneel on the mattress,
and poke my face through the curtains.
The moon is full, spilling across the fields,
and pooling in the garden.
And — there!
What is that?

A chill up my spine at the movement.
Is that the mist or —
No, no, that is a lady.
I see her walk through the mist,
her dress pools behind her.
She steps a little strangely,
like I did when I was first learning how.
But her arms raise to the moon,
and they are slender and strong.
Like Mama's.

Slowly she turns,
the mist around her train kicks up and swirls
She is looking at me, I think and I—
I am not afraid.

Margie stood in the garden, where the moonlight limned her mist in brilliant silver. Yes, stood. Not on feet, for the mist does not have those. It does not have the perfectly articulated joints and tapered bones that allows for gentle steps. But she raised herself to the height that felt best, gave herself shoulders and a neck, let

her mist billow behind her like the fur humans named hair. She let it curl in the humidity, a wild and lovely thing that spun as she turned. Then Margie used her mist to clothe herself, in wide, long skirts to cover her lack of feet. She imagined them strong, of cotton and wool, something she could wipe the soil on after a day of hard toil.

Once the image was formed, she pushed herself forward, trying to glide, to mimic in her mist clothes the way hips and thighs sway in gait. She toppled and wobbled, and it reminded her of children in their first steps. This made her chuckle, and the roosting birds in the rafters of the abandoned cottages flapped their wings.

Margie reveled in the moon's kiss upon her shoulders; she raised her arms to embrace it, the way she remembered the women have done in the centuries before.

A rustle and gasp came from the cottage behind.

Margie pivoted, careful to keep her shape intact, careful to keep the mist around her absent ankles.

Aila.

Aila in the window, the moonlight highlighting the curve of her still full cheeks, the pucker of her lips as they hang open and betray the origin of the gasp.

Margie wonders what the girl sees in the garden.

Does she see the mist at play, a faulty attempt, a vain pretend?

Margie starts to feel what you might call foolish. Of course, of course the mist cannot be a human. She knew that. Of course, of course she did.

But then Aila — Aila smiled. She raised her hand and, barely perceptibly, moved it back and forth. Margie remembered this, remembered this was how humans greet each other. They don't do this to the boar or the deer, they don't do this to the stream or the clouds. Only to one another. Human to human.

Margie focused. She pulled her misty arm up, formed fingers from it, and flailed it back and forth in the way she'd observed. She must not have done it quite right, because Aila chuckled. Promptly she was then pulled down from the window ledge by what must have been the arms of no-longer-sleeping parents. But before she passed out of view, Aila smiled. Smiled at Margie, just as the humans do after a shared greeting.

If Margie had skin, she would have come out of it for the joy of her ruse.

I'm playing by the stream today.
The sun is warm on my back,
but the water is so very cold.
My toes perch on the grassy ledge,
but the splashes still reach them.
I have a stick, and I'm poking
at something I see glittering.
Glittering beneath an already
shimmering surface.

I stretch and poke harder,
That sound! Is it metal?
Papa is in the field nearby,
while Mama is gone over the hill
to waulk wool with the other women.
Would Papa know what this metal is
buried here, within the stream?

I poke it again and the sand moves,
the water billows it up and pushes it away,
and I see it.
A steel emblem,
a circlish shape.
I'd step in and pick it up,
 if the icy water wasn't so biting.

Finally, I scoot it to the edge
where my stick can scoop it up.
Silt is stuck in the edges so I scrub it clean,
in the reddish heather.
The grey steel is blackish in parts,
but I can see the shape now.
A flower, like the little roses that grow
around the banks of the stream,
and I see shapes on the bottom
that might be letters.

Papa will know what it says.
He reads really good. I wish I could.
"Papa!" I yell as I run between the buildings.
Mama said they all used to have people in them,
our family, long since scattered.
I don't like the empty houses.
Their windows are like eyes that watch me.
Their doors swing open on their hinges
like yawning mouths.

I tell myself they're just sleeping.
But it doesn't stop the chill up my spine.

Papa says it's a good thing,
that now we have more places to store the crops,
more food to get through the coming winter.
I can't remember ever filling even one house with food.
Sometimes, when my tummy growls,
I imagine each house filled with grain
so much that it spills out the doors
and we don't have to be sad for the spoil.
That makes the empty houses less scary.
For a moment.

I round the last one and can see Papa bent over the fire,
throwing in more kelp to be burned.
I hate the smell and, as I get close,
I cover my nose with my elbow.
I have a treasure to show him.
"Papa! Look!"
He calls me his little one,
and asks what I've found.
I hold it out proudly.

"A right treasure! It was in the stream!"
But Papa's face changes
when he turns the steel rose over in his hand.
His eyes get sad.
Why are his eyes sad?

His jaw sets like he's angry.
Why would he be angry?
Did I do something wrong?

His hand closes over the pin tightly
and then he looks at me.
The lines on his forehead change,
less angry, more sad. Why sad?
He sinks to one knee in front of me.
He says it's a great treasure, but he's sorry,
I cannot keep it.
He says it's very old,
but some people would be upset if they saw it.

"I'd keep it a secret!" I say,
and I feel the excitement of my catch twist.
"I just want to look at it!"
He says he knows,
and that it is special that I found it,
but we cannot hold onto it.
He offers to melt it down,
so I can keep the steel
But I don't want the steel.
I want the metal flower.

Papa gets sadder when I start crying.
But I can't stop.
I don't think I'm crying about the metal flower,
I think I'm crying because everything special

is slipping and I'm hungry.
He wipes some of my tears,
with the hand that isn't keeping my steel rose.
His fingers are rough on my face.
When I look up at him, I see a shine down his cheeks.
Is he hungry too?

But the kelp has burned out,
the ashes ready to spread,
and he must return to his work.
I head back, past the empty houses.
The wind blows through a window,
the door squeaks open.
And it sounds like someone crying.
I hate it.

I pivot toward the trees where Mama takes me.
Maybe I can find some mushrooms.
Maybe that will make Papa happy, and
maybe that will make my tummy less sad.

Margie floated above the bones.
Bones. Bones in her woods.
Human bones.
For all of the remains Margie has seen in the eons in this glen, none were human. Those bodies were always planted in the garden before the land could take their flesh. She'd never seen their structure before, and this — it felt wrong to see this. Felt wrong

that whoever had owned these bones had not been planted in time to feed the soil.

Why hadn't they been planted? The bones lay here within the underbrush. The jaw slack as if it had been open when the air's gift was rejected. Why were the bones here? Whose were they?

Yet, for all of its wrongness, Margie could not look away. She traced the shapes of the bones, and couldn't deny that she wondered if she could use this new knowledge, if it would help her perfect her human mist structure. She set to memorizing it, the way the bones fit within each other where the cartilage was not yet dissolved.

Margie started her experiment.

First, she pulled herself to the height most common in the women.

Shoulders, neck, head, hair. She'd work on facial features later. Arms, elbows, floppy fingers.

No, no.

Those should not be floppy.

Margie leaned forward and studied the bones, the connections, the way they fit. Then she formed her mist. First phalanges and metacarpals. Then misty flesh.

She splayed and twisted them.

Yes, yes. This was right, Margie thought, and she marveled at the feeling. She knew they held no strength. No, she still could not lift a spear to hide it, or carry a child, or revive a drowning woman.

Still, for just this moment, Margie reveled in pretend.

Now for the feet.

She did not yet clothe herself in misty dress, so she studied the column of water droplets holding up her formed top half.

First, legs. Yes, split the mist in two.

Thighs and skinnable knees and shin bones that hurt while growing.

She liked to add the backstory. It added to the illusion.

Then the ankles, the complicated delicate fit of bone on bone, angles engineered to perfection. Now the tarsals and metatarsals. You know these as such, reader; obviously, Margie does not. Still, it helps for me to translate to you.

Margie stood fully formed and naked. Can the mist be naked? The human body is so incredibly formed. Like the slopes and dips of the land, both strong and soft. Why do they feel shame in their nakedness? Or, Margie thought, maybe they don't. Maybe they only wear skirts to wipe off the dirt when working. Yes, yes, Margie was sure that's right. Still, she was not working, and she was too proud of her new legs and ankles and feet to cover them.

That problem resolved, it was time for the ultimate test, the test she'd seen performed by every young human for hundreds of years. The wiggle test.

Margie the Mist Sprite wiggled her toes.

And, sure enough, they displaced the soil and sunk in. Of course, the dirt did not bury her feet; it couldn't. It filled her water droplets and dirtied them, and Margie cared not a bit. She felt — she felt alive. 'Toes' in the soil, just like the children, just like the remaining mother when she looked for mushrooms and knew no one was around to care.

Margie was around. Margie cared. Margie cared quite a bit that the woman felt safe enough in her grove to let her toes dig into the earth that will hold her after death. Yes, yes. This was right.

Margie wiggled her toes deeper, and with her misty senses she felt the tree roots talking, felt the mycelium growing. For a moment, all was well.

But then the mycelium quivered.

The tree roots whispered.

The forest delivered the news.

As quick a summer storm Margie returned to just mist, for her child was alone in the grove.

The Child and the Bones

The woods are scary without Mama.
Normally Mama sings.
She takes off her shoes and stockings at the edge,
and wiggles her toes into the grass with me.
She steps into the forest, and it welcomes her,
the trees rustle so it sounds like clapping,
and I think they want her here.
I don't think they want me here.

The trees are quiet, standing still.
The whispers are gossips.
There is no wonder and I am afraid.
I step a little further in,
thinking maybe the woods would welcome me
if they knew me.
Could they know me?
The trees are still.
Where is Mama's friend?

Her mist, her *cheo*?

Where is our friend?

Margie sped through the woods, following the stillness of the trees. They did not often like the humans watching the evidence of their communication.

The unmoving trees led Margie through her woods.

And there she found her, the little girl crouched near the ground, eyes wide and frightened.

Frightened.

Margie slowed her spread, wove gently, naturally. Disguising herself this time in her natural form she shows with the mother, disguised as just the mist. Just the mist.

She settled low to the dead leaves ready to become nourishment, and approached the little girl as casually as possible. Just the mist.

Just the mist watching its daughter.

Not wanting her to be alone, worried she'll be frightened.

Hush, reader. Of course it's a normal thing for the mist to do. Yes, Marge. You're doing great.

Margie came around the curve of the log. Aila had pulled her knees into her chest, her head burrowed between them, elbows crossed to cover her face. Margie took this as a sign to fill up the air, to let the little girl feel her more than see her — willing her to feel the cool kiss of the mist on gooseflesh skin. Why do they call it that? Margie has always wondered. The only geese she's seen are far more feathery than fleshy; she cannot imagine them bumpy like the humans get when chilled or frightened. Sure enough, the skin on Aila's arms grows raised and bumpy. Hopefully chilled, not scared. Please don't be scared.

Margie pretended to hold her breath, imagining what it might be like to have breath to hold. The trees' stillness added to the silence, and no birds rustled their feathers.

After another century passed (it was only a few seconds, but it felt like forever to Marge whose heart was held by a little girl who had no clue she had power to move the mist itself) Aila lowered her arm and twisted her head to peek over the edge of her knee. Margie watched her track the whitened air, the way the dark forest looked a little brighter.

Aila blinked.

Blinked some more.

Rubbed her eyes with tight fists as if to clear them, and squinted as if into the bright sun.

And then, in a moment that Margie wished she could live time and time again, her Aila said,

"Oh! You're here!"

She came.

Mama's friend, she came!

The trees are still scary,

but they're a little brighter now.

And the birds started rustling again,

chirping here and there.

The forest feels alive,

feels like when Mama is here with me.

I like that it thinks I'm like Mama.

I want to be the forest's friend, too.

How does Mama do it?

How does she talk to it?

"Hello," I start.

I sound little, afraid. I don't want to, though.

Mama never sounds afraid, but she's so big.

I sit taller, straighter.

What can I tell the mist that makes me sound grown up?

What can I say that will make them like me?

"I found a treasure today!"

I can't help how excited I sound.

That's probably okay.

Treasure is exciting for anyone.

I think the mist got thicker, closer,

just like it's listening.

It must be working; I sound like Mama.

"I found it in the stream.

It was glittering under the water,

and I pulled it out with a stick."

Margie leaned in, enraptured by the girl's story. She was talking to her. To her! Margie could hardly believe it, and tried to stay as still as possible, refusing to be the reason her Aila stopped.

Margie marveled at how the little girl spoke like her mother. She told Margie about the treasure in the stream and how excited she'd been about it. Margie could imagine; she'd be excited if she found a treasure too. But as Aila began to describe her treasure, her voice started sounding sad. Why would she be sad? A discovery is no small thing.

The thought of a discovery pulled Margie's thoughts back to

the bones in the woods. She didn't know why they were there or whose they belonged to.

Maybe the girl would know.

And as Aila continued to talk about how sad she was to lose her discovery, Margie thought maybe she could fix it.

The mist starts to move.
Did I imagine that?
I wipe the tear that slips down my cheeks,
and look again.
No, it's real.
The mist is now a tight line,
stretching deeper into the forest.
Mama had told me the mist was leading us,
Back when the mist had looked just like this.
So, just like Mama,
I follow.

Margie led the girl deeper into the woods. She had been quite proud of her idea to replace Aila's discovery with a new one. She was even prouder that the girl had realized what Margie was doing and followed her easily.

But as Aila tripped over roots and stumbled over rocks hidden by the ferns, Margie started to doubt the quality of her plan. When the girl fell to her knees, Margie wished she was made of something Aila could hold onto. When Aila sat back, her bloodied knees exposed to Margie's own mist, Margie wished her game of pretend had been something of substance.

If she pulled herself into her womanly form, could she carry Aila home? What would the parents do, seeing their daughter held in the arms of something so weak? What would Aila do if she transformed? Would she like her as much as she did when she'd seen her in the garden?

Her fingers are less floppy now; would Aila be impressed?

But then Aila got up and pushed ahead, ignoring the red water bubbling up with each bend of her joint. Margie leaned in, kissing her mist into the wound, hoping she could do something to clean it and protect it from infection. She hoped Mara would be proud.

And yet, while Margie's mist was concentrated this closely, Aila shivered.

Margie had almost always loved her coolness, loved how it protected the crops from the sun, loved how it kissed the mushroom caps. Now she wished she was somehow different, wished she could lean in to warm and comfort. The humans seemed to love warmth shared with each other in embraces and cast plaids over the shoulders (before these dark days, of course; there is no plaid in sight now).

What would it be like to be warm?

Margie realized she didn't know the feeling, never had.

No, when the bonfires lit up the nights she'd stayed away. The flames repelled her, even when she wished she could draw close, even when they licked up Mara's stone still body.

But now Margie imagined what it would feel like to have a body that accepted warmth, shoulders strong enough to hold a plaid. Would her misty fingers disappear if she splayed them before the fire as the humans do? Would the heat change them, melt or boil — would she lose the frame she'd so intentionally crafted?

Margie had to halt her wondering as they approached destined piece of forest. The forest with the body, the body that's only bones. The trees were silent here, even to her. The birds didn't chirp, and only one occasionally let out a mournful, keening cry. The silence screamed that this was wrong, that bodies are supposed to be planted or returned to the land in a different way. Not left like this, not so exposed.

When Margie saw the jaw lying slack, the bones and teeth separated in an eternal scream, she stopped.

And then, Aila screamed.

She screamed, a sound of terror Margie had only heard on the darkest nights, had hoped in earnest she'd never hear again. But here it was, the scream in her woods. And it was her fault.

Mama and Papa are talking.
They think I'm asleep.
I've tricked them so I can listen.
They're talking about the bones I found,
the bones the mist led me to.
I was so scared.
It felt so wrong,
some ghost from Papa's stories,
screaming at me.

I didn't mean to scream.
Still, I couldn't help it.
I screamed and screamed until Papa came.
He scooped me up and held me tightly,

A Mist Sprite's Study of Being Human

He said I scared him. Said he couldn't find me.
He said it was hard to see in the mist.
It's never hard for me to see in the mist.
Is that because I was born in the mist?
That's what Mama always says.
That's not what Mama is saying now.

She's talking about another family,
another house over the hill.
She says they had to leave their home,
something about a fire?
I don't understand.
Papa asks about the taxes,
I don't know what that word means,
but it makes them both afraid.
Why are they afraid?

Papa asks about the shore,
says maybe it's better to do it on our own
than to be forced.
Forced to do what? Forced by who?
I wish I could ask.
I wish they'd tell me.
They wouldn't tell me. They think I'm too small,
they think I'm not strong enough.
But I carried the basket to the forest by myself.

And then today I spoke with the mist,
I followed it just like Mama,

I tried to be just like Mama.
Maybe I wasn't very good at it.

Mama and Papa stop their talking
as the candles go out,
and hold me closely between them.
When Papa snores I don't laugh.
I'm still too scared.
There's a bird ruffling it's feathers outside.
Maybe the lady is in the garden.
I don't look,
I'm still too afraid.

Margie wished she could take it back.

From the first scream to the moment she saw the man's face, she knew she'd made the wrong choice. This was a bad idea. His strong arms had no problem picking up his child and holding her close, running his fingers through her hair as he soothed her.

Margie wanted to do that so badly. Why couldn't she be strong enough? Why couldn't she hold closely the ones she loves? Well, she's just the mist.

Over the coming Babylonian weeks, a new sound emerged from the woods. It was the sounds of crying and wailing, of old songs in old tongues, leaded down by the weight of too much loss. When the songs ended, Margie would find more bones, more bodies ready to be planted.

And no one around to do the digging.

Margie had never felt so weak.

Her people had never felt so afraid.

The Mist and the Flames

Margie avoided the woods because of the songs and the wandering men, the ones who should be in their own glens with their families and hearths. Margie couldn't bring herself to hear them, to watch them wander into their own form of wildness. She had seen nothing like this. No, when the elderly were pulled to an odd sort of wonder, a strange reversion to childhood, they were supposed to be with their families.

They were supposed to be with their families.

Margie couldn't stay, couldn't watch. It was so unnatural, so wrong. She let the elders grow quiet in the woods and you could say she felt badly for it, as if she was betraying some deep instinct that had grown around her particles which urged her to watch, to care.

But what was the mist to do? Burying the flowers over the raised earth of the first grave was one thing; the water was strong enough for that and the seeds had done the rest (as evidenced by their annual emergence throughout the stone garden). But Margie could not dig, could not even lift the handle of a shovel. She had considered leading the remaining glen father to the bodies, but she wasn't sure if he'd follow her like his mate and daughter had — especially since that day with Aila.

After the forest discovery they'd been careful to keep Aila close. Even the mother barely skirted the edge of the woods for mushrooms or berries, staying always within eyesight of the cottages. They didn't know why the body was there, and they didn't want to welcome more trouble by disturbing it.

Margie had observed this ebb and flow among the generations. Some held odd beliefs about this kind of thing, but those beliefs sluffed off in future generations before eventually returning. It's like the tide, Margie might offer, if Margie had ever seen the shore. But Margie had never seen the shore, which you might think odd for an eons-old being on a small island.

And if you do, then I'll ask: have you ever been to Scotland? Because while it is, yes, a small island in a lovely sea, the land feels so large to someone bound to the soil. You can so easily become lost in glen and loch for eons, without ever finding the cliffs and waves. While it seems small from above, it's bigger on the inside. For a content and curious mist sprite like Margie, there had not yet been a need to venture as far as the sea; all she'd ever wanted was right here.

But right here was changing. She'd seen the tide of change splash against the distant hill, spraying its mist into the bowl of her valley, tainting small things here and there over the years. Of course, of course things had changed in the 25,700 or more Babylonian weeks since that first big change. (Namely, the humans starting their shelters here. You remember that, right? Making sure you're keeping up; we've covered a lot of ground.) But, just like beliefs, change had ebbed and flowed even before the humans came. Dry spells were followed by floods, oppressive heat by oppressive cold. Nature had a way of finding the balance, even if the swing seemed extreme to someone limited by time. But Margie was not limited by time, and so the pendulum swing, as you might call it, did not seem so extreme to her. It was easy to wait it out when you would live for eternity.

Something about these changes felt more foreboding – the once-full glen with only one family remaining, the empty cottages with yawning mouths. This felt different. When nature changed, the evidence was taken back to the earth. A fire took down a swath of trees? The soil took the nutrients and grew from it. The stream flooded its banks? The flattened grass and debris would eventually straighten or be broken down and grown around.

The stone garden permanently changed the land. Would that be grown around? Margie couldn't imagine so. And what of all the cottages? The plots for herbs, the long strips of tilled land? Although she remembered what it looked like before, Margie could not picture all of this being just one side of a double-edged change sword. No this was development, growth. The trees don't grow just to shrink again. The mist doesn't learn feelings just to unlearn them.

But what of the bodies in the woods? What of their haunting songs and the screams before their silence? Would this just be a blip in their experience, like the burning women and clanging of shields? But the clanging and the burning had changed Margie. She took those losses into herself and carried them. They sit right next to her love, her love for Aila and the rest of them, her love for the trees and mushrooms and waters. Does love hold space for loss? It seems like they are sisters, sitting together.

Margie continued to ponder this as she stayed close to the glen, watching over her little family, avoiding the wood wanderers. She watched the father slump over his tools when he thought no one was looking, watched his jaw harden as he returned to work. Margie watched the mother's gaze grow distant when she squeezed Aila close.

What did Mama know?

What does Mama know?
She squeezes me tighter these days.
She doesn't let me step into the woods.
When we hear cries, she tells me it's only the birds.
It doesn't sound like the birds.
And when she thinks I'm not watching,
her face falls for a moment,
and she looks sadder than sad.
What does Mama know?

What does Papa fear?
He squeezes me tighter these days.
He doesn't like when I pull away to play.
When I jump at the sounds and look to the woods,
he tightens his hold on me.
Just for a second.
He doesn't say it's the birds.
He doesn't lie to me.
But sometimes it's harder
to see the bald truth on his face, and I wonder,

A Mist Sprite's Study of Being Human

What does Papa fear?

What does the mist whisper?
Mama's friend stays close on the edge,
tight to the mountain,
avoiding the trees.
Just like Mama,
away from the deep woods.
When I think of the mist I see the bones still,
they scream at me in my dreams.
But when I wake and look out the window,
the lady is walking in the garden
and she's doing a better job of it now.
She walks and she whispers.
Of what does she whisper?

What do I see?
Behind the mist lady,
up the road to the hill?
Little sparks dancing,
bugs reflecting the hearth light?
They're moving and maybe growing.
Getting bigger? No,
closer.
They wag and they waver.
The lady in the garden whirls to me,
and it seems she has eyes now,
landing on me, wide with fear.
What do I see?

"Not again," Margie thought as the hands holding fire descended the road, closing in nearer and nearer to her family's homes. She was standing in the garden, tall, supported by mist calves and metatarsals, when she heard the shuffle in the window.

Aila, her Aila, was watching the torches. Did she know what they meant? Did Margie? She hadn't perfected her facial features yet, but she felt the first learned feeling quiver through her drops, and she wondered if Aila saw it, if Aila knew the word for fear and could name it in the mist's watery eyes.

Though they had not buried women in the water in many hundreds of weeks, it was the first thing Margie thought of. Were they coming for this mother, to bury another? Not again. Never again.

Margie's thoughts raced. Could she convince her sister waters to reject the women's presence? Could they float her atop where the air's breath could still reach her? Or could Margie wrap herself around the woman, would that protect her somehow? What could the mist do?

What could she do?

When the first torches reached the first house, Margie knew this was different. They did not hold a book or use words to explain their decisions. They did not need a group gathered in witness. When the roof of the furthest house was licked by the flames, Margie saw. She saw their plan, spreading out across the valley's floor, each torch headed for each house.

And Margie could not do nothing. Not now, not again.

She dissolved back to her misty form and the sharp gasp in the window punctuated the end of her ruse. She set that loss aside and spread herself wide, filling the glen as fully and thickly as she could. She rushed for each house, filling the thatch with as much moisture as she could manage. The first one lit was already too dry, and its heat pushed back her moisture, the smoke clogging her particles as she withdrew from it.

As the roofbeams fell with a snap like bone, the mist remembered every bairn born there, the first mates who built it, the family cart as they left the croft behind. Made frantic by the new blaze, Margie pulled water from her stream sisters and poured every bit she could back into the remaining roofs. If she could scream at the sky sisters she would.

Willing, pleading, for them to drop their rain.

They did not.

They floated by, even clearing enough to let the stars watch as the sparks lifted to them, the ashes of memories with them.

And Margie would never forgive the clouds for it. For the rest of her eternal existence she would stay near the earth, abandoning the heavens for its rejection on the night the cottages burned.

The Child and the Basket

The lady in the garden collapsed when the fireflies spread.
I don't know where she went,
but my gasp woke Mama.
She smelled something then.
She woke Papa, who jumped with a start,
and threw open the door.
I see his silhouette there now,
the misty evening blue a halo around him.
But there — what's that?
A splash of orange, like a twirled skirt.
Another flash, yellow and hot.

Papa turns to us, his eyes wide
just like the lady in the garden before she left.
Will Papa leave too?
Mama's up now and scrambling,
Papa holds her face still,
hands on both cheeks,

keeping her eyes on his.
He says something to her I don't understand.
He kisses her on the forehead,
and tears run down both their cheeks.
When he looks at me, it's almost a goodbye.

I won't let him say goodbye.
But he's gone,
out the door toward the sounds of cracking
and the smell of smoke.
Where is the smoke from?
Our hearth fire burns small.

I'm holding the basket,
Mama said it's important that I help hold the basket.
She put some blankets in it.
They're wrapped around small treasures.
I think of my small rose.
I would have put it in the basket,
if I still had it.

Mama puts more in the basket,
some dried food, an old book.
She asks if it's too heavy,
and I'm strong so I tell her, "No."
And she believed me,
because I did a good job
lying.

The father was yelling at the other men who weren't listening, who continued their spread, lifting their torches to thatch, and lowering them to garden plots. Margie worried for the stone garden in the corner, but they hadn't seen it yet. She thickened her mist on that edge of the cottage grove to hide it.

Though her moisture in the thatch initially worked to slow the spread of the flames, soon the building heat in the valley was drying out the air faster than she could replenish it. She was growing weak. She could tell her mist had shrunk under the oppressive cloud of dark smoke blocking the star's view. Good. Margie would rather they not see. They had no right to watch.

A little girl's scream drew all of Margie's attention.

Aila. Her Aila.

She pulled in all her mist for strength, and sped along the ground back to her daughter's cottage, the only one now without a fiery cap. The men had a grip tight on Aila's arm, pulling her from the cottage, tossing her to the packed earth. Then they grabbed the mother, who flailed and screamed and kicked her legs in the air. Margie felt then she could never even pretend to have that kind of strength. When they threw her to the ground next to Aila, she immediately turned to hold her daughter. Because she had the arms. Because she could.

What could the mist do as the child and her mother huddled in the grass, sparks falling on their skirts from the gathered torches and building flames? That was it. She pulled herself lower and laid herself across their skirts, willing the moisture protect them from the flames.

And from here, covering them with herself, she watched as the father yelled with the men. He begged and pleaded, saltwater making rivulets down his face, washing the dark ash in streaks, striped like a wildcat. Finally, he must have gotten what he wanted for the other men nodded.

She didn't understand when the other men gathered around the roof, when they started tearing down the thatch and wood beams. The mother started crying then, and Aila just sat, wide-eyed, as unwise to the events as Margie. The men lowered the main roof beam, dropping it to the ground where the father hoisted it onto his back and carried it over a shoulder away from the stone walls. As it passed, Margie remembered the tree, this first one toppled when the first family settled here. For all of these sunrises and sunsets it had canopied these humans, a shelter in death as much as it sheltered the deer and boar and skittering squirrel while it still had branches to rustle. And although it had now been dead for centuries, it had never felt more lifeless than here on the ground, still and motionless, as the world went up in flames around it.

Margie didn't understand.

Didn't understand when they still set fire to the inside of the house, to all the places her humans had laid and sat, drank and ate, laughed and cried. She hadn't been inside the houses but she'd seen through the wall holes, heard through the cracked doors and in the smoke from the chimneys.

Aila didn't understand either.

Since she first landed on the grass, she had barely moved. Had watched stunned, had sat silently. But when the flames engulfed the curtains, she suddenly moved, jumped up, knuckles white around the handle of the basket she wouldn't drop. She ran for the house, as if she could stop the flames herself, as if a child had any power over the whims of men with torches.

Papa caught her, of course. His strong arms were perfect for it. But he hadn't been able to lift her before her foot landed on one of the fallen embers. When she screamed out, the sound was a pain of flesh and pain of soul. Margie hated it. She knew the father did too, for his gaze upon the other men was just as heated as the coal that burned his daughter.

None of the emotions Margie had learned equipped her for this. There was anger, yes. Fear too. She knew she only felt these because she also felt love. But that love was a heat in her particles now. It felt she was burning from within like these walls of exhumed stones.

Margie had also learned the feeling of longing, and she felt like that was mixed in here somewhere, only twisted, somehow. Sharper. Longing for things as they were hours ago, and knowing, even this close, she is already further from that time than she ever will be.

All of the past's goodness turned to ash.

Eventually the father placed Aila back on her mother's lap, her burned feet on the skirts that Margie was shielding. She wrapped a cold kiss around the blisters already forming, and was thankful to have this gift to give.

They sat there all night, watching the house give in to the flames' whims. It cracked the bones and boiled the insides, until all that was left when the sun rose was an ashen pit of their before. Yes, forever onward, just as Margie split time by before and after the humans came, time would split here too.

Before and after the night of flames.

The sun was red and orange when it broke over the hill and

through the dense smoke. Margie thought it looked like blood, and was glad it, at least, understood.

The sun looks like a drop of blood,
like the blisters on my foot,
like the red under Papa's eyes,
like the flames I see
every time I
blink.

Mama hasn't spoken.
She rocks me
like when I was younger,
I didn't ask her to do it.
I am not younger.
But I think she needs it so I
stay.

Our house is gone.
The walls are still there,
the stones too strong
But Papa says even they won't stand long.
I don't know why
they burned our
home.

We still have the cart.
They didn't burn the wagon or wheels,

so Papa attaches it to the donkey
and with a groan
sets the wooden beam
inside.

Mama lifts me up.
She sets me on the cart,
I sit next to the beam,
between the blankets and things
she'd grabbed before the flames,
and I hold my
basket.

We are going up the road.
The cart is bumpy up the hill,
I jostle all around as we climb,
the houses getting smaller
behind us as we go.
And still
I hold
my basket.

Margie's humans were leaving.

They loaded the old tree into the cart. Then Aila beside it, and
Mama next to Papa as he led the donkey up and up and up the
road. Soon, too soon, they would disappear over the edge, out of
sight and far too far. Far too far.

Margie stood in the middle of the still smoking ruins, and no
piece of her particles had room for the knowledge she needed to

grasp. It was over. They were going. Going. Her daughter of the mist, her friends, her family. Her humans she had learned to love. Leaving. Over the hill with the first tree their ancestors felled.

And she was watching them go.

No. No. She could not watch them go.

She could not watch one more bad thing happen to them. She could not find solace in the quiet. Already the birdsong haunted her, the happy chirps and rustle of leaves felt wrong against the sullen scene.

She had tried last night. She had tried.

But what could the mist do? She was just the mist.

Just the mist, protecting skirts from sparks and soothing burnt flesh.

No, it seemed all she could do was done up close.

And they were going far.

She'd miss the trees and mushrooms, miss the grass and slopes, miss the streams and falls. She'd never been over the hill. But her heart was going, so she would too.

The mist came up the road,
slow and quiet, near the earth.
Like it meant to sneak.
Like it meant to join us.
I'm no longer afraid of it
leading me off into the woods.
There are bigger things to fear now,
than bones in the trees.

The mist is coming closer still,
but waiting for permission.
Mama wouldn't mind,
I'm sure. It always was her friend.
But how would it travel with us?
How would it stay close?
My hands are tight around the basket
and I lift it just a bit.

Come, come, mist.
Come gentle friend.
Come hide right here,
inside my basket.
I'll carry you with me
wherever we're going.
I'll carry you with me
inside my basket.

The Mist and the Salt Air

On a day unlike any other, Margie found herself inside a basket.

She would not normally fit inside a basket, of course, but she couldn't deny Aila's request. In her weakened state from the heat and smoke pollution she was able to condense herself down, eager to find a place within the things they'd saved. For many hours this piece of self perched atop a ceramic jar, careful not to make the blankets too damp.

While this small piece perched, the rest of her skimmed alongside the road, just within the tree coverage. It's not that she didn't want her humans to see her. She just didn't know what other humans might say.

She was going to meet other humans.

Some had come into her glen over the eons, of course, of course they had. They came for rituals or foraging or hunts. They came to scope out land for homes for themselves. And then, after this family was established, they'd come for celebrations or feasts, to help with the farming, help with the loud bringing forth of life, or stand by as the family planted the dead. Other humans had come to bring news, or proclaim judgment. They came for Mara. Then men came to train, and the ones in red came for pain. She was well accustomed to the idea that there were more people out there on this land than just her family.

But she'd never been to those glens. She'd never seen them in their own fields.

And after the men came the night before to burn her cottages and gardens, she wasn't sure she wanted to.

Her feelings had grown so large in last few years since Aila was born, but in the wake of the flames, Margie felt herself closing in. Her thoughts often turned to the smoke and screams, to the snapping structures, the sullen sighs. So much, too much, gone like that.

And now she was going, she was gone, gone over the hill away from her moss-capped rocks and fallen trunks, gone from her sister waters and their raging falls. The things she kept were not the things she wanted. Her indifferent sky sisters sill floated above, unchanged from the night's events. The songs of wood-wanderers also remained with her, haunting from deep in the forest.

Margie stayed close to the tree line, hoping her frailty would lend her an air of invisibility. This was a fabulous pun in many ways, as you know. She does not understand our humor; even if she did, she's not quite in the laughing mood. No, our Marge is sullen and sunken, slipping and slinking undetected through the brush that did not yet look too different from her own.

But she knew it was different.

You could say she knew her glen like the back of her hand. And that would be silly because she only barely knows that. No, she knows her land far, far better. Every rise and dip, every curve and hollow, from the highest slope to the deepest creek bed, she has all of it memorized. And for every piece of heather and waving grass here that looked similar to her own, the differences were even more obvious.

No, no, this stone is not hers. Her moss-capped stone is a little dented on one side, a little like a thumb was pressed into it when large hands broke down the edges of the mountains and scattered them.

No, no, this creek is not hers. Her bubbling creek has a lower, deeper tune. It warbles while the higher sisters wibble.

No, no this tree is not hers. Her tree had more red to its bark, and when the branches spread they felt like arms asking for an embrace.

No, none of this was Margie's glen. It was good, still, I guess, sure. It was still similar, at least. But the similarities felt pointed, sharp, a twisting of the new feeling that had sliced into all the internal organs she imagined were essential.

Do you know the name for this feeling, reader?

It's like longing, she knows, but bottomless. Like finding your feet are no longer on the ground and you might yet fall forever. It's a dark pit inside your stomach which whispers you know exactly how to fix the problem, and yet cannot. Perhaps never will.

Our Margie is homesick.

Homesick after only a few miles away from the glen. But if you'd lived in one spot for eons of an endless existence, I'd imagine you would also feel homesick whether an inch or a world away from that spot. And sometimes being an inch away feels further because you're almost there, but you can't go back.

So close, yet so far and all of that.

Margie could go back, of course. Of course, she could. But her people wouldn't be there. Her daughter wouldn't. After the events of the burning night, she can't imagine roaming those blackened, smoking ruins alone. It wouldn't feel right.

So no, she was not turning back. She was pressing on through the ever-changing slope of the land, further away from the slicing pain, learning to make a home in herself for the feeling.

When she heard the distant waves, the tide's ebb and flow she'll finally get to see, Margie tried to feel excited.

Mama calls it the ocean,
that's the big line we see
as the cart rolls over another hill.
The line stretches to the left and right
it cuts the sky in half
and I can't understand any of it
except that it's loud.
But Mama is excited to show me.
I try to be excited too.

Papa stops our cart by a new group of houses,
newer yet looking older
and squished so close together.
Mama takes my hand and pulls
toward the ocean, toward the sound.
She's got a smile on that I know
isn't her real one.

A Mist Sprite's Study of Being Human

Her real one breaks across her face
like the sunset over the hill,
it warms her whole face and it's
not like this one.
This one I recognize now,
she's worn it more and more
in the last months,
since the bones,
since the screaming.

This smile is for me, I think.
A smile a mother gives her child
 when she'd much rather cry,
but doesn't want her child to.
I don't want this smile,
I want the old one.
But I don't know
when I'll see it again.

So I smile back,
and I wonder if she realizes
mine is new too.
The smile of a child,
who would much rather cry,
but knows Mama doesn't like it.

We wind through the buildings,
and the people.

So very many people.
So very many sounds.
So very many smells.
And I don't think I like it,
but I follow.

Then we're at the edge,
the grasses turned hardier,
sharper, stronger
until they turn to stone.
Is that what the ocean does?
Already the wind whips harder.
My hair blown back and forth across
my cheeks until they feel worn,
raw,
rock.

Will the shore do the same to me?
Will I have to get stronger,
stiffer, sharper?
Will all my squishy stuff
turn cold,
until I too
am hard
as the stones,
under my feet,
which I glimpse
between the
whipping strands?

Mama asks me to look up,
 as she crouches down to me
and pushes the hair from my face,
her soft hands
holding it back
as they cup my cheeks.

Mama is still soft.
She points at the line and turns to see it,
but I don't want to turn,
to see the sharpening sea.
I want to keep watching my soft Mama,
lest she too
is turned to stone.

Margie perched atop the slope that slowly became the sea. Between her and the eternal line separating sky and the salty version of herself were a dozen cottages, all hobbly and bent, squished far too closely. You, reader, might imagine it like a cramped cemetery that had long since run out of room. One where the older headstones were leaning, and the newer ones were not much straighter. But Margie would not understand the connection. Her stone garden in the glen was much better tended than this.

And between every building, winding down each path, were humans. Dozens of them, so many Margie could hardly believe it. She'd seen hundreds of humans in the 25,706 weeks (give or take) since they permanently set up home in her glen, but never this many all in one place. The most she'd seen at once were when the men were preparing for whatever conquest they later embarked on. The one from which they never returned. Margie's droplets seemed heavier with the weight of these memories, these losses she's tucked between her particles, forming a sort of beating heart within her (if you could believe it).

Something about seeing so many humans in one place made her feel further away from home than ever. They all had a sullen look to them, heavy and forlorn. She wondered if they had burning nights of their own, if their origins were stained with as much smoke. Margie could not find another reason for why so many people had chosen this one spot to live. There was only one small bubbling sister water on the edge, the soil looked like it was unsuitable for crops, and the rocky surface of everything made it seem hard to imagine gardens. She saw a couple of plots, but the drooping yellow leaves only further confirmed her hypothesis. No, this land was not fit for this many people. Could they drink the sea? Is that why they were here?

Margie wished she could see it, could see where Aila and her mother had run off to. Would the sea explain this odd choice? The air smelled of brine and she recognized the seaweed odor as soon as the cart crested the final hill standing sentinel to this coagulation. The glen father had often burned the kelp and spread it on his fields, coaxing life from them when the nutrients were scarce. By the strength of the smell, Margie began to understand this is where the kelp came from before it was scattered over fields near and far.

But the kelp didn't help these drooping garden plots.

Does the ocean have other gifts to give, other hopes to offer?

She decided then that she'd find a way to the ocean for the answers she sought. But, for now, she whirled and craned, looked for the father and the cart, the basket safe inside.

They'd pried it from Aila's hands when her mother smiled and led her towards the shore. It looked like her fingers had been stiff when she finally released it, sore from gripping it so tightly through the night and their journey here. Margie had been sure to leave the small piece of self in the basket until Aila was out of sight so she wouldn't be afraid she'd left her behind.

But now that Margie was wholly back together, the small lent piece seasoned her misty form with the smell of blankets and jam, ceramics and papers — tiny bits of the home they'd left behind. She wasn't ready to accept that it was gone. But perhaps they'd carve out a home here too. Perhaps they'd make room for her.

Margie stayed to the edges of the village, low and slow, a passing spit of mist to anyone watching. But no one was watching, reader. There were too many pressing, boring things to steal their focus. Isn't that how it is? When was the last time you let nature distract you from your work? Have you seen the mist sneak past you? Perhaps it happened and you just weren't watching. You get my point. There were clothes to be washed, and kelp to harvest, and gardens to groan at while you wring your hands in your skirts and wish it all was better than it is. So Margie made it around the outskirts to an uninhabited hovel with no roof to keep out the sprinkling rain. The glen father was talking with the other men, his hands on his hips as he looked at the vacant air above the stone perimeter of a not-yet home.

When his hand landed on the wood beam still resting in the cart, Margie realized his plan. For all of their journey she wondered the purpose of carrying the old tree that had long sheltered their family. Now she saw the mercy he'd been granted. Margie watched as the other men helped hers lift it up and into place. They built the rest of the roof around it, resting beams in its old slots and connecting them (albeit precariously) between the stones in the perimeters. It looked to Margie like an exposed ribcage. Margie can draw that connection now she's actually seen an exposed ribcage. She didn't like the feeling it gave her, to see the wooden skeleton laid over the scant home for her family. Would it cradle them? Would it protect them? She feared not.

She hoped so.

The men clothed the bones with flesh of thatch, and then they scattered, her glen father left alone at the doorway of their new home. Margie watched as he rested a hand on the door frame. It was the motion she'd seen in grief, a hand laid on the shoulder of a friend, a recognition of the loss made lighter by companionship. But then his shoulders bent in and shook. When new salt seasoned the damp air, Margie understood.

For the lifting of a wooden beam over a shoulder, the carrying it over hills and hollows, the fitting of it in a new roof in a home not yet their own — this was strength. Of course, of course it was. But while Margie watched weeping bend his shoulders low and shake them, she heard a familiar call.

"Papa!" came her Aila, running through the streets.

The father transformed then into a greater strength, his heavy grief turned to pauldrons on his shoulders, his white knuckles on the stone willing it into a shield. When he pivoted and bent, arms stretched to collect his daughter, his smile was a helmet visor dropped. Margie was thankful, then, as the man brought his daughter and her mother into their new home, that his arms were strong enough to hold them; there was more than the old bones of trees sheltering her family in this new, salty place.

The Child and the Sea

I miss our old home,
though each day I forget a little more.
I squeeze my eyes shut to listen,
willing my ears to block out the ever-calling tides
and the screech of the soaring guillemots,
trying to replace them with the memory
of rustling pines, the giggle of the creek.
But the sound in my mind is distorted, wrong.
Like a poem about something the writer
had never seen.

But I had seen it.
Once upon a time I lived in a valley
hugged by mountains, watered by streams,
surrounded by forests, fed by its brambles.
Yet that life is fading in my mind,
replaced by the constant sounds of
people and animals

quarreling and weeping.

The phantom feeling of fullness in my belly
is a ghost come to taunt,
to be swallowed up by the aching hunger,
the gap of this tattered tunic
where it once fit right.
The seasons have come and gone,
Year folded into year,
and as time pulled its tax,
it took the food too.

I see the concern in Mama's eyes
when she holds my thinning face
in her mussel-worn hands.
I see the tick in Papa's jaw at my state,
and at her fear.
But there are no mushrooms here.
No brambles or berries.
And the cockles that once kept us sated
have disappeared under the reach
of too much hunger.

But once I was a friend of the mist.
She stood in the garden
and shook hands with the moon.
She danced in the forest
and led us to its fruits.
I try to forget the bones,

the screaming, the smoke in the night.
The flaming sword that sent us out,
to make room for sheep's clothes.

That's why they took our home,
I learned. The sheep wanted it.
They wanted our grasses and heather,
they wanted the moss and clover.
But what of the glade and its coolness?
What of the stream and its secrets,
did they want those too,
or would they be left abandoned?
If they wanted the mist, they couldn't have her
for she had come with us.

But she doesn't stay close.
There is not space for her in this pile
of stone houses and cobbled walks
rotting kelp and dismal plots.
Sometimes I pause while hanging the clothes
to watch her pacing
always off on the side
past the alleys and byways,
keeping low and woven,
between the wind beaten reeds
at the edge of the sea.

On the rare days
when the tide grows quiet,

I think I hear her crying.
I look away to allow her dignity.
For I know what it is to not be able
to hold the tears in,
while everyone wonders
why you aren't yet hard enough
to fully forget your home.

Mama is calling to me,
something about time, about evening.
Something about packing the basket.
I feel an old ache in my joints,
in my fingerbones, whatever they're called,
that still remember how to wrap tightly
around all we can take.
I tear my eyes away from the mist.
I don't bother asking if she will fit.

The basket is lighter than I remember.
I tell myself it's because I'm stronger,
and that muffles the screaming
in my throat,
in my chest,
in the flutter under my skin,
because I do a good job
lying.

Margie watched the ebb and flow of time take and steal. She'd tell you it was like the tides, seeing as she can draw that connection now, but there's too much bitterness in her particles for her to find pride in that. For the ocean had not yet revealed its secrets to Margie even though she had been careful to stay still and listen. It had not yet told her why it gathered the people to itself, and it had not shared its plan to protect them, to feed them. She couldn't imagine it was as indifferent to their plight as her sky sisters, but as its coming and goings droned out a constant rhythm, she feared it really would remain silent, foaming and roiling, deaf to the cries of those huddled along its curves.

But Margie heard them.

She heard the fathers' voices raise, in anger and in fear, as more exports were turned away, as recompense never came.

She heard the children as they grew silent, their cheeks sunken, their voices weak. On her misty dress she could feel the echoes of their soft tugs on their own mothers' skirts, reaching for a solace always past their grasp.

She heard the mothers' wail as their little ones were lost to their hunger, as a new garden was filled with small stones. It grew beside a sharp building pointed upward, reaching for her sky sisters, learning from them how to turn its face away from the cries of grief.

So Margie begged the ocean. She kept vigil on the emptier edge of the coast where her presence disturbed as few as possible; though occasionally she felt the gaze of familiar eyes. But the thought of Aila, growing ever older on this harsh jut of land, only made Margie more focused, only strengthened her resolve to study this strange water that somehow mirrored in itself humanity's toil and calm, its ability to be both soft and sharp. She couldn't believe the sea to be indifferent, when it seemed like the beginning and end of all their stories.

She begged the ocean to lend its ear, to offer up its crops, to protect the ones given to its care, and added to it her own salty waters in hopes of making proper payment.

I stand on the rocking wooden boards.
There is no room for us inside,
beneath the deck where I might
close my eyes and imagine myself safe and warm
 between the walls of my old home,
where the mist walked the garden.

No, the sun has brightened the sky enough,
from behind the curve of the earth
to see the grey skies that watch us,
that threaten rain to come
that, were we home, would tell me to
bring in the washing,
and hope for mushrooms.

Mama squeezes my hand,
I don't think she meant to do it,
or that she did it for me.
As I look at her face I think she did it
to know I'm still here.
I squeeze back.

She won't take her eyes
off the line of sea and sky,
but she bends to lift me
and settle me on her hip.
I'm not yet too big,
and she's not yet too weak.

"Look, Aila."
And I follow her gaze this time,
what more can the ocean do to me?
So I see what she sees,
a green hill suspended
between the sea and
sky.

Margie had continued her pacing of the shore through the night, just as every night before, only distracted for a moment by an irregular wave pattern interrupting the otherwise steady lapping and breaking down of the shore stones. As she leaned in to watch, she thought she heard echoes of something — some change, some resilience. She thought the tide perhaps had begun to listen, and that's what it was telling her with this broken rhythm. She held tighter to that old pesky hope as dawn illuminated the thick blanket of sky sisters wrapped in grey. Margie felt she had the evidence to allow herself that one moment of hope, for in the last few weeks more and more wooden housings floated on its surface toward the sky-splitting line, and that had to mean something. Margie didn't understand what the ocean planned, but perhaps there was a garden just past the horizon where it would answer all their cries.

Perhaps those who left would fill their bellies, returning with gladdened hearts.

Perhaps they'd bring new food with them, and ways to revive the long-drained land.

Reader, take not for granted the gift of inhabiting the future, of reading a past story and knowing what is to come. For while a pit grows in your stomach at the inevitable rolling of history's wheel and you put together the clues (if you know anything of the mass-emigration of the children of Scotland), Margie does not know to fear the signs. She does not know that what she thinks is a lent ear and a gracious acquiescence will soon steal from her the very reason she makes these requests. She does not know that this strange tide is the wake of oars, and the rough disturbance of departure.

Perhaps, reader, you are also making requests. For while you look to the past for this story and, gifted as you are with historical hindsight, can guess how it will end, you are also inhabiting a present. In this present, you are equally ignorant as to what might be ahead of you.

You may be standing on a shore of your own, pleading with indifferent skies and droning tides for solace and comfort, for a metaphorical *light at the end of a tunnel.*

For what it's worth, I hope you get that.

I hope, for the first time, that you are not like Margie.

I hope when dawn slinks across the dimming stars and you listen for the familiar padding of a child's steps in stiff grasses you are not met with mere silence.

I hope you do not wander through abandoned streets, as

Margie did.

I hope you do not find yourself waiting for smoke to billow to the skies from a familiar roof, only to see indifferent sisters floating by, unmoved by the lack of rising incense from a cold chimney.

I hope you, unlike Margie, find yourself closer to a hopeful light at the end of the shadowed, damp places.

For our Margie finds herself in a new kind of darkness as she watches a spot disappear between indifferent sky and bitter sea.

Our Margie, once alone in a glen she loved, finds herself alone again, unable to look away as what she has learned to call home sails further than any misty arms could reach.

On the green hill,
I think I see a flicker of white,
a float, a wisp.
I dig into my eyes with a fist,
blinking away the sea spray,
trying to peer through the violent rocking
crackling of boards,
which remind me of the rattle
of the ceramic jar, in my basket
on the back of the cart,
leaving our glen.

I think back and try to remember.
Did the little jar crack
when we went over the holes?
Did it shatter on the bumps, or did,

No - the mist was there,
perched atop, nestled within.
I swallow against the ache of her absence
and shove down the feeling
of being a fragile jar,
in a rocking basket
with no mist to cushion the break.

Papa comes up beside Mama,
wraps an arm around us,
and by the way he squeezes
the meaning of this voyage
settles deeper into my chest,
seeping into the bones that
calcify and harden, finally, into stone.
I'm not too young to recognize a goodbye.

Our boat rises and falls over the ocean's hills,
a new kind of mist spraying across our faces.
Its bitterness so different from my *cheo's*,
that I can't hold back my own salt
which leaks down my cheeks.
Mama squeezes me tighter
what else could she do?
And I squeeze back,
because what else can I do
as I blink back the final feelings,
and am forced to watch our home being eaten
by that eternal line.

The Mist and the Villages

On a day just like the recent others, Margie wandered vacant paths.

Not all of the humans had left on the big ship that took her family from her, but most had. The ones who remain wandered as listlessly as Margie, lost to their hunger and the silence that overtakes a soul when there is no one to hear them.

In those first days, the remaining ones thought they saw the ghost of a lady walking the shoreline. They thought they saw her reach graceful arms to the surf, her head tilted back to face the sky, mouth wide in a wordless scream. They thought they saw her collapse to her knees, too smoothly to be real, incorporeal fingers plunging into undisturbed, sea-smoothed stone.

So, when she walked the paths, no one paid her any mind. At first, they shook their heads to clear their vision; now their minds made room for ghosts around every corner.

The ghosts of homes once filled, long burned and left.

Ghosts of family farms once bountiful, now left untilled.

Ghosts of young and old, lost to the unyielding land.

Ghosts of ships on the horizon, ever suspended, neither coming nor going.

Ghosts of ghosts. What was one more?

Margie wandered as the days bled together, sunrises already sunsets.

She noted the emptied crofts, more still emptying, a steady drip from the wound at Scotland's side. She noted the small gatherings at the edge of the church yard, more plots in the hard ground than people left to witness. She noted the gardens long abandoned, and she remembered with a sharp fondness the first time she laid herself low over a plot like this. There was no point in protecting these gardens. There was no one left to harvest them.

There was another change Margie noted.

At first, when the ships were still visible on the horizon, her misty form had come easily. It lent her a frame within which to sort her many griefs. It felt right to be in the shape of a human when her heart, if she'd had one, was breaking. It felt right to have shoulders to bow and shake. It felt right to have cheeks to swipe saltwater from when it seemed no one was looking. It felt right to open up to a passing sky with a scream that sounded like a howl of wind through the mountains.

But as the bleeding wound leaked its people into the sea or soil, pushing them ever past her misty grasp, it grew more difficult for Margie to form her misty shape. The angles were wrong, the joints stiff. At first, she thought it was just a new way to carry her grief, but soon it was impossible to ignore.

Still she wandered, hobbled and bent like the vacant homes with yawning mouths, eyelids open. For no one was left to close them.

One day, when she stretched her hand for a bent reed, no fingers formed.

Another day her feet were so malformed there were no toes to wiggle, none to sink into the cold soil.

And on her final day in the village, there was no slender neck to stretch, no shoulders to drape in a misty shawl, no skirts, and no hands to wipe on them.

It was then she noticed the complete silence.

She wound along on the ground, in her old misty, ambiguous shape, until she found her; the final elder human, left alone and cold above the ground. Breath stood by, arms dropped to its side, knowing its gift would no longer be accepted here. The human's vacant eyes were locked on the skies, and if Margie could form the words she'd say,

"They won't see, dear. They won't answer. They won't care."

No, only the air and mist stood vigil at this final passing, far from the church yard and the other cold stones. No, here the final human lay, exposed to uncaring skies. Margie wished more than ever she could lift the dirt, a blanket, a pile of rocks. She did not know the name of this human who chose to live out their final days on the isle of her birth, preferring to pass on familiar soil than wherever the ocean had taken the last of her children.

But Margie could not lift stones or cloth, she could not even gather herself to lay low over the woman, watering her skin one final time with the mist of her homeland. Margie was slipping, slowing, her mind slogging through a million stored things and recognizing few of them.

All she knew then was that she needed to go home.

Home to the glen, where she always was and had been.

The glen would know her.

The forest.

The sister waters.

The strong mountains.

They'd restore her strength. That's it.

She'd just been gone too long.

But as Margie began the trudging slog up the road to the hill that had become the sea, she thought she might be feeling something.

She just couldn't remember the word for it.

~~I'm still on the boat.~~
~~We're a long way off~~
~~floating on a sea of~~
~~"Not yet"~~

~~And as the sickness spreads~~
~~the bodies are cast off~~
~~into the foaming mouth~~
~~of the sea,~~

~~I begin to wish,~~
~~if this must be my end,~~
~~I could have passed in the grass~~
~~'neath the heather~~
~~with the mist.~~

~~"Land ho," they finally call,~~

~~and those of us with strength left~~
~~stagger to the rail.~~
~~A large green dot~~
~~splits the sky and sea~~
~~and my tired soul wonders still~~
~~if a new mist~~
~~waits there~~
~~for me.~~

The mist barely remembered the path to the shore from their glen, but something old took over. Margie found herself rising higher than she let herself in the past ages, skimming the tops of trees, pulled by a force more natural than she'd been in a long while.

The mist moistened the crowns of the pines as the waves of the land rolled. Below her she could make out songs of some remaining wandering ones, and though she did not want that to be a familiar thing, it brought back a bit more of her usual self.

The mist passed over towns of less and less people.

She passed over more and more abandoned crofts.

Margie heard the screams of those experiencing their first burning nights, and the memory of her own was dislodged from between her thinning particles. Smoke and ash, a crying girl, skirts Margie can't remember why she was protecting.

When Margie passed peopled places, it seemed she was able to reach her old memories and vocabulary. She was sad, right? She thought that was the word for it. That was a word for her feelings as she watched forced clearings and more burnings, farms after farms still smoking. She was shocked by the lack of trees, forests spread thin and thinning. For a moment she was able to feel a sense of gratitude to the first glen son who propagated the young pines in her glen, and taught his young to do the same.

When she saw corpses with ropes around their wrists, bodies thinned from endless hunger, she felt something else. Anger, was it? The word felt strange on her not-tongue.

The further out the mist went, the quieter it grew. No smoke from village chimneys. No conversations around cold, lonely firepits. No cries from newborn babes, no giggling children. No sounds of toil and labor.

As the mist traveled on, the silence closed in. Occasionally, here and there, came the sounds of scattered birdsong, squirrel skitters, the brushing of branches as the trees talked. But even these seemed to still as she passed, as if aware of a grieving force of nature who had forgotten the words to name her distress.

If she could remember the words, she'd think, "I just have to make it to the glade. It will remember me. It will revive me."

And as she neared a crest in the land, a rise making way to a familiar hollow, she may have thought, "Yes, yes. I remember this. I'm almost there." But even those thoughts were wibbly, washy, see-though.

The last thing the mist heard as it rounded the final bend toward a glen long hers, was the bleat of an unfazed sheep.

we found a place and it's okay.
but the mist is different here.

III

THE MIST

The Mist in the Stone Garden

The mist perched atop the ridge on the road worn down by people she used to remember. Could she? Remember? Perhaps if she sucked in and held her misty breath just right, she could make out some shapes. A head on shoulders, arms and legs to hold the frame. The faces are a blur of centuries, some features keeping siblings through the eons, others smoothed out to conformity. The ghosts of these people drifted past her on the path, and she tried to recognize them, to call out to them.

Was that the song of their voices on the wind? A hush, a giggle, a mother's comforting murmurs. A father's hum as he bounces a new bairn. The sounds are right at the edge of her particles, just barely out of reach, as if the origin had gone past earshot and all she's hearing are the remaining vibrations in the air. No, no, maybe it's just a trick of the wind.

From her promontory, the mist took in the old glen she'd once known better than the back of her hand. (Of course, she doesn't remember that either.) As she tracked the forest's movement, the sister waters burbling, the high mountains still and low grasses waving, the mist felt like this was right.

This was where she belonged, where she's always belonged. She felt a pull toward the tree line, though she couldn't put words to it if we asked her. Some base nature tugged her from the path. Why is there a path, anyway? It was too wide and worn down for the deer to have made it. And the foxes don't like to feel predictable. Path, that's a weird word. Say it enough times with a misty tongue and it turns into a sound. That's it, just an old sound. The mist left the sound behind and moved further into the glen.

And were those rocks always there? Stacked in odd piles, making shapes she felt she should remember. They haunted her, the way they're stacked and stumbling, half solid and half broken. Something about them was familiar. Yes, yes, they looked like the sides of the mountains and their boulder crumbs. That's it. How odd, stacked stone mounds in the middle of her glen. It used to be empty, didn't it? She searched her memory particles for the origin and found a blank space.

The mist couldn't find the memory.

She couldn't recall why the rocks were blackened and smelt of acrid smoke.

She couldn't remember why the soil around them was blocked out in squares and angles, wooden tools discarded and disintegrating.

She couldn't remember why the earth itself hugged the old buildings this way — paths softening out now, eaten over by heather and tromped by new beasts.

She definitely didn't remember the sheep.

No, these mostly silent, land-dwelling versions of her sky sisters were grazing glumly on the grasses here and there with no logical course.

They hadn't been here before, she didn't think. Not this many, not like this.

She passed by one and it peered up, its glassy, slitted eyes looking her over before going back to its meal. Unbothered by the passing spit of mist.

Was that all she was. All she had ever has been?

I can't tell you how many hours passed while our Margie wandered the vacant glen, tugged between natural instincts and fading recollections.

If you had been in the glen that day, you would have marveled at how the mist hung low and sat in the valley around old ruins and grazing sheep. You may have even stopped to take a photo of it, for a pretty picture it was, if you don't think about how deeply sad it all was. But perhaps, if you were in the glen that day, you might not have known why it was sad. With a deep, contented sigh you would have captured a new image worth treasuring and turned back to your path. I don't mean to guilt you; it's not your fault, after all. But I will tell you, if you knew, and if you stayed, you may have seen quite a sight.

For while Margie sat dumbly in her ancient homeland, a bell was rung on the south end of the glen that led down to another set of fields. The sheep looked up and around, but upon deciding the summons must not be too urgent, went back to grazing. This meant the old shepherds had to come looking for their stubborn fuzzy bastards. They crossed the rise and may have thought, "My, what pretty mist this evening."

But at the vibration of a human heartbeat, Margie stirred.

Margie awoke.

Her glen, she was in her glen.

These stones, the old homes.

Blackened from the burning night.

That path worn down by the rush of children at play.

That stone removed after stubbing too many toes, skinning many a knee.

That water where her women were taken.

The hill where her daughter was born.

Aila, that was it. That was her name.

Aila and Mara and all the other mothers and fathers and daughters and sons passed before Margie's memory.

She remembered the human hearts whose rhythms had pumped water and blood through their veins, whose tongues formed ancient words and filled the glen with a magic powerful enough to name the mist, to make her believe she might be more than just a low-lying cloud.

The sheep bounded past Margie toward the lone shepherd atop the hill. She watched him glance over the vacant valley and crumbling crofts, and she thought she saw sadness in his exhale, grief at the corner of his eyes.

But then he turned and started back the way he came. With his every step away, Margie felt the slowing of her soul, her heart if you could call it so.

Fear. That's what she felt first as her already sluggish thoughts realized what was happening.

Then it was longing, longing for things to still be the way they had been.

Anger came next. Anger for all she'd lost, all that had been taken from her.

Resignation was next, with a deep-seated hollow hopelessness.

When this man finally left with his sheep, what would become of Margie? Would she revert to the semi-sentience of before the humans had moved here, kept slightly afloat by the distant beating of human hearts and the occasional wise woman passing through?

Margie feared this time would be far worse, for though she had once been alone in this glen, the Highlands were never so vacant, so devoid of the undercurrent of human heartbeats as she observed on her pilgrimage here. If it was their rhythms in the soil that kept her from being as indifferent as her sky sisters, what would happen this time, when the draining land had dripped away its final sons? Margie's thoughts were slow—slowing now, difficult, to g—

to grasp.

She twisted and looked around,

panic and fear f—

f—

filling the last of her particles.

If this was it, where did she want to sp—spe—

spend her en—end?

And then she knew.

She had no time n—

now.

No time, but still,

she p—

pushed and p—

pulled along the ground,

against the atmosphere's attraction,

against her nature's base call.

She t—

turned instead to the corner yard,
and st—
stretched and scr—
scr—
scrunched her way
across the trampled gardens
and overgrowing p—
pa—
paths
paths paths
until she made it
to the stone garden.

Margie touched each stone in turn (if you can imagine this with me, reader, it will give her a bit more strength). Margie touched each one and pulled herself along with a misty grasp that almost resembled fingers bent with age caressing the top of
well-worn,
well-tended headstones
in a garden well-loved
by its family.
The mist pulled itself deeper, and if you'd been on the edge of the glen that evening you may have thought you'd seen the ghost of a woman haunting the old graveyard. You may have thought she was whispering her goodbyes to each stone in an old tongue long since lost to colonization's centuries. You might have been enraptured by this; maybe you would have stayed to watch as she reached the oldest stone, lichen-loved and darkened by age. Perhaps you would have been confused to see the ghost bend then,

folding and dissolving. Maybe you would have blinked and shaken your head, peeling your eyes wide to peer through the darkening night to make out any shapes. You wouldn't have been able, if you were on the edge of the glen that night, to see the mist lay herself low across the old grave. You wouldn't have been able to translate the whooshes and pitters and pats of the trees and bird songs.

But I can tell you, reader, that as the mist laid low on that first grave of the humans who taught her the names of feelings she'd soon lose, her droplets were filled to the bursting. The same love that long ago spread her over this plot in the hope it would bear fruit, that was the precipitation gathering on the rough old stones, causing rivulets along the loamy earth, seeping deep down to sing itself into the mycelium and tree roots and broken-down old bones.

The clouds passed silently above, parting just enough for the moon and stars to highlight the silver mist as she chose to water the earth with her love rather than pass untouched above it.

Reader, if you were in the glen that evening, perhaps a chill would have run up your spine at the silence and the song in it, drawn in by the rhythms of deep love and outstretched arms. Somewhere in the pulsing heartbeat of branching roots and spreading organisms you may, if you were in the glen that evening, have felt in the silence an indescribable cry. In the gooseflesh on your arms, you may have wondered at the somber howling, and the draw in your soul to wander into the glen. To call yourself her child.

But you, reader, are not in the glen.

No. It is finally, and woefully, empty.

And though the mist would have loved to spread graceful arms to welcome you, how could she?

She is just the mist.

THE MIST ALONG THE PATHS

143

FLIP PAGES TO WATCH TIME PASS.

A Mist Sprite's Study of Being Human

The Mist Within the Ruins

147

The Mist Over the Waters

152

The Mist Amidst the Heather

155

The Mist Beside the Mushrooms

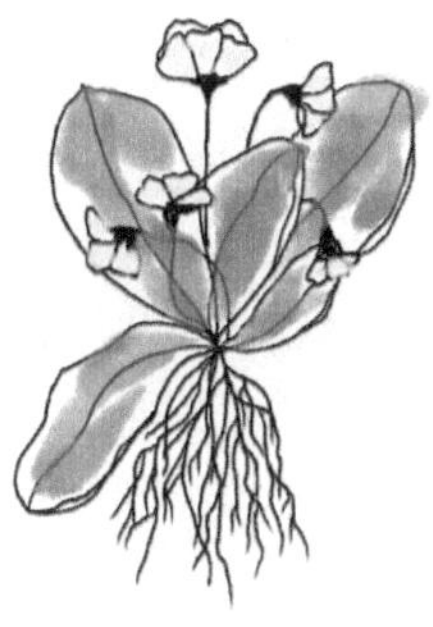

The Mist Within the Trees

The Mist Atop the Heights

A Mist Sprite's Study of Being Human

170

171

173

The End

Epilogue

The boughs q-qu-quiver,
a tremble beginning in the deepest
twining and tangle of roots
and it f-f-feels like, it reminds me of
f-f-fingers squeezing another's in warning,
in anticipation and I w-wo-wonder
if the other is squeezing back.

I learned the talk of the trees,
an eon ago when I studied at their base,
where bark breaks soil and forest decay gathers in witness.
In my despair I tried to burrow as deeply as I could
into the soil at their f-f-feet
and hoped they would let me
slip away into p-p-peace
even with no st-sto-stone to mark
my resting place.

I shiver and feel the rattle of
frozen particles
of late winter
fractalized in my being
And it seems like – something.
Like crackling, yes. But not of twigs.
Not of fire – an age-old f-fl-inch takes me
something my waters remember,
something I can't
Name.

Bones!
No, no — joints.
That's the crackling, that's
the feeling in my droplets
as something stirs.
Something is stirring
in me.

I peer through the bleariness,
swipe at the pine needles in my face
in this place I've been resting,
where I've been floating,
obscuring the tops of the trees.
It became too hard to stay
near the ground.

Now I p-pu-pull myself down,
g-g-grasp over misty grasp,

on these a-a-arms that tethered me
and kept me from being
only a passing cloud.

No, for all that slipped
through my h-h-hands,
And all that feels missing
from my moisture,
I kept my promise.
I didn't let the sky have me.

And now,
as I st-str-stretch back
to the forest floor to ask of the roots,
and the rocks,
the mosses and mushrooms,
what is it that has them trembling,
what is it that granted me this moment
of sentience?

A sudden hush, a stillness,
Twined root fingers squeezed tightly,
held breath.
Breath. Yes.
I let an exhale loose
and it frosts the mushroom nearest me.
I gi-gi-giggle as I dust it off,
as I nuzzle it, hoping
it understands my apology.

A Mist Sprite's Study of Being Human

Somewhere
birds take flight,
and when I look up,
I catch the eye of a doe.

She looks through me, into me,
into the thing that used to beat,
that still feels tugged like sk-ski-skirts
when young birds and pine martens
keen for their mothers.

This mama looks into my soul
all the scattered, tattered bits,
losses only a mother knows,
and she dips her head.

When she turns to track a sound
I fe-fe-feel it
Not just stirring, but b-be-beating
a rhythm long absent.

I can't hold myself back.
No, I lean deeper to the soil
'ears' pressed to the dirt,
'hands' splayed,
'fingers' burrowing down.

Is the smell of loam returning my words?
I ask the roots, the mycelium, but no.

This song is not theirs, this steady drone.
Ba-bum
ba-bum
ba-bum ba-bum.

My head shoots up,
quicker now than I've been able to move
in so many sun visits and moon phases.
In so many w-we-weeks.

'Weeks' is not a long enough measure of the time
Since my thoughts came to me so easily
traveling between these trees,
so swiftly, in and through me.
But now my thoughts
are forming up from the frost,

Unfurling, unbending,
they face me, ghosts of ghosts
and I think they're asking
for permission.
To come back, to come home,
to awaken this old soul which
pain rocked to sleep.

Crystaline c-cl-clothes hang from their frost forms.
The memories I know belong in me,
the ones I'd stored away
for safe keeping.

One more beat,
one more pause to decide.
No, I can't. But -- yes.
Yes, it is time.

I pass through them,
and as each is engulfed in my mist
I shiver with remembrance.
With grief.

Blood and flames,
scraped knees and
drowned screams.
Frosted spears and
flowered stones.

I stand now before the final frost ghost.
I s-st-stand. I—
I look down at my feet.
Feet!

Ankle joints articulated; toes buried in soil.
And when I look back up to this final memory,
I see
her.

Formed from white spits of the mist I'd left behind.
My Aila, my child of the mist.
As she was last time I saw her,

thinning, tamed, and sea-sharpened.
Yes, yes. I remember, the curves of her cheeks,
her eyes wide and wild.
Her knuckles white around a basket handle,
her knee bleeding as we passed through the woods.
Her first words, her first steps.
Her giggles at my own first faltering gait.

I don't walk much better now, I'd long forgotten how.
But I p-pu-push myself forward.
I s-st-step, and st-st-stretch
out a hand, for a cheek, for a child
long mine, long lost.
I form eyelids for myself just so I can close them
just so I can prepare for this last bit of self
to return to me.

A gasp,
Not mine.
Misty eyelids fly open
And before me, no
Not Aila.
This woman
formed of flesh and color,
hair whipping in a real wind.
Eyes wide with wonder.

The Beginning

Timeline &
Historical References

Because the worst parts of this story are true.

Margie & the Glen

(PRE 1100 C.E.)

At one time, Scotland consisted largely of dense forest. The end of the last Ice Age saw the beginning of the reign of the trees; various species made up Scotland's ancient woodlands, including rowans, birch, oak, elm, juniper, yew and Scot's pine. The land was also home to many other species of plant and animals. Red deer, red squirrels, pine martens and otters would have dominated the brush, while Capercaillie, osprey and owls ruled the roosts. At this time, red squirrels "could have hopped, skipped and jumped between branches from Glasgow to Aberdeen and beyond without coming down to the ground." ('Scotland' magazine)

Margie & the Headless Pine

(AROUND 1319 C.E.)

Scotland's forests flourished until the first trees were felled by settlers around six thousand years ago. (Scotland's Forestry Strategy

2019–2029) The land has since suffered great deforestation. In 2024, the vast majority of trees in Scotland are planted and felled for timber; just four per cent of Scotland holds native woodland. (NatureScot)

MARGIE AND THE LAND BREAKERS
(AROUND 1300-1350 C.E.)

The Highlanders of this time were a trusting, welcoming people who believed strongly in community. A black house – aigh-dubh in Gaelic – housed animals as well as people. (Historic Environment Scotland) The inhabitants associated locked doors "with inhospitality and meanness," believing they "had a moral obligation to welcome strangers and provide hospitality for friends and neighbours." (Am Baile)

MARGIE AND THE SONGS
(AROUND 1350-1500 C.E.)

Plague blighted Scotland's population between 1584 and 1588 and again between 1597 and 1609. While recorded evidence of the plague in the Highlands and Islands is sparse, historical evidence of folk remedies for the symptoms suggest it was prevalent in these areas, too. (National Library of Scotland)

MARGIE AND THE BURNING ONES
(AROUND 1500-1690 C.E.)

Scotland was swept up in the second wave of European witch hunts between 1590 and 1662. (Martin) When, in 1590, King James VI and his fiancée, Anna of Denmark, were caught in a wild sea storm, he proclaimed witches were responsible and his fixation on eradicating this threat was sparked. Between four and six thousand prosecutions took place in Scotland, four times the average in Europe. (Henton)

As well as many methods of torture to force false confessions, accused witches were often subjected to the water ordeal, being bound and thrown into bodies of water. If the sank, they were proclaimed innocent, but they often drowned; floating was regarded as proof of witchcraft and they would be executed, often burned at the stake. (Mackinlay)

Margie and the Broken Tongues
(Around 1700 C.E.)

Many in Scotland starved to death between 1695 and 1699 – referred to as the seven ill years – due to extremely poor harvests. Primarily affecting Northern Scotland, an estimated five to fifteen percent of the population were lost, though in some area the death rate was as high as a quarter of the populace. (Cullen)

English soldiers – redcoats – took up residence in garrisons across the Highlands from 1725 to enforce English rule and tackle resistance to King George I.

Jacobite rebellions sprung up all over Scotland; the last and most violent was led by Bonnie Prince Charlie in 1745 and 1746. The Battle of Culloden ended this revolt. 'The Act of Proscription' was passed the following year, outlawing clan tartan, the playing of bagpipes and the use of the Gaelic language. (Steves)

Margie & the Ones Who Stayed
(1747 – 1808 C.E.)

In the time of peace following the Revolutionary War and

the Napoleonic War, British finances were thriving. Highland landlords ended the longstanding tradition of tenants paying rent in kind. Unable to pay cash, Highlanders were evicted from their homes – which were often burned or destroyed to render them uninhabitable – and the land was rented to sheep farmers for grazing.

Tenants, forced out of their clan territories, moved closer to the shore to work in the fishing industry or harvesting kelp. This period marked the first phase of the Highland clearances. (MacInnes)

Margie and the Leanabh a' Cheo,
The Child and The Mist,
The Mist and the Garden
(1808-1813 C.E.)

Brooches depicting a steel rose were commonly worn by Jacobites; these symbols, like tartan, became dangerous to possess after the defeat at Culloden. (Dreid)

Kelp farming became integral to life for crofters; they carried heavy loads from the shore, often up dangerous, unsafe paths to fertilise fields. (Price)

The Child and the Bones,
The Mist and the Flames
(1813 C.E.)

Landlords dispelled their tenants as swiftly as possible in favour of flocks of sheep, which were far more financially lucrative. (McConville) This was often violent, as "bayonet, truncheon and fire were used to drive them from their homes." (Prebble)

The trauma of displacement caused intense psychological distress, particularly for older members of Highland communities. Some wandered the land until they died of exposure. Some report hearing singing from the woods. (MacKenzie)

Some Scots refused to leave their ancestral homes and hid in the remains of their ruined villages or in pits and hovels in the earth. They had little or no access to food or shelter, many surviving on potatoes alone. Those who survived this ordeal were forcibly removed. (Blamires)

The Child and the Basket
(1813 C.E.)

Some tenants were able to salvage supporting timbers from their homes and take them to new sites to rebuild a dwelling. This was seen as an act of grace. (MacKenzie)

An eyewitness to the clearance of the Badinloskin settlement describes a hundred-year-old woman present in a home to be burned: "I informed the persons about to set fire to the house of this circumstance, and prevailed on them to wait till Mr. Sellar came. On his arrival I told him of the poor old woman being in a condition unfit for removal. He replied, 'Damn her, the old witch, she has lived too long; let her burn.' Fire was immediately set to the house, and the blankets in which she was carried were in flames before she could be got out. She was placed in a little shed, and it was with great difficulty they were prevented from firing it also. The old woman's daughter arrived while the house was on fire, and assisted the neighbours in removing her mother out of the flames and smoke, presenting a picture of horror which I shall never forget, but cannot attempt to describe. She died within five days." (MacLeod)

In 1821, the Duke of Sutherland commented, "Strathbora is now effectually Cleared of all its turbulent people. The removings were completed on Friday night and the houses demolished without a single word. Some are off for Caithness but the bulk of them seem to have a wish to go to America. We are now I think settled for a few years." (Blamires)

THE MIST AND THE SALT AIR
(1813 C.E.)

Rents continued to rise. In Skye, for example, rent was increased seventy-five per cent from 1799 to 1803. The Crofters Act was passed in 1886, promising homes to displaced Highlanders if they worked the land they rented and paid sufficient rent. (McConville) New crofts, often on the shoreline, became available to displaced people; these crofts were purposefully built in areas where it was impossible to make sufficient profit from the land to pay rents:

"Many of their allotments, especially on the western coast, were barren in the extreme—unsheltered by bush or tree, and exposed to the sweeping sea-winds, and in time of tempest, to the blighting spray; and it was found a matter of the extremest difficulty to keep the few cattle which they had retained, from wandering, especially in the night-time, into the better sheltered and more fertile interior." (MacKenzie)

THE CHILD AND THE SEA
(1815 C.E.)

The kelp industry collapsed and was no longer profitable. Tenants were often forced to eat the seaweed they once sold to survive. Starvation was rife. (Day) The people who had once thrived on the land "became amphibious, and, as an English author says, lived half on land and half on water, and after all did not live upon both." (Marx)

The Mist and the Villages
(1815 C.E.)

Between 1770 and 1850, approximately two hundred thousand Highlanders were forcibly evicted from their homes. (Steel) More than seventy thousand people emigrated. (Dimond) Some villages were entirely eradicated. For example, Balnabodach's 1851 census reveals that every person living there in 1841 was gone. ('The National')

Some families fought hard to stay on their land. In Suishnish, for example, thirty-two families – around a hundred and fifty people – were cleared three separate times, in 1849, 1852 and 1852. An eye witness describes one of the families taking shelter in "a wretched hovel, unfit for sheep or pigs... William Matheson, a widower, took ill and expired on the following Sunday. His family consisted of an aged mother, 96, and his own four children - John 17, Alex 14, William 11 and Peggy 9 - the old woman was lying-in and when a brother-in-law of Matheson called to see how he was, he was horror struck to find Matheson lying dead on the same pallet of straw on which the old woman rested; and there also lay his two children, Alexander and Peggy, sick!" (Balmires)

Others were forced to emigrate; Archibald Geike describes a scene in 1854: "I could see a long and motley procession winding along the road that lead north from Suishnish. It halted at the point of the road opposite Kilbride, and there the lamentation became long and loud. As I drew nearer, I could see that the minister with his wife and daughters had come out to meet the people and bid them all farewell. It was a miscellaneous gathering of at least three generations of crofters. There were old men and women, too feeble to walk, who were placed in carts; the younger members of the community on foot were carrying their bundles of clothes and household effects, while the children, with looks of alarm, walked alongside. There was a pause in the notes of woe as a last word was exchanged with the family of Kilbride. Everyone was in tears; each wished to clasp the hands that had so often be-friended them, and it seemed as if they could not tear themselves away. When they set forth once more, a cry of grief went up to heaven, the long plaintive wail, like a funeral coronach, was resumed, and after the last of the emigrants had disappeared behind the hill, the sound seemed to re-echo through the whole valley of strath in one prolonged note of desolation. The people were on their way to be shipped to Canada." (Balmires)

The Mist in the Stone Garden
(1815 C.E.)

"All was silence and desolation. Blackened and roofless huts, still enveloped in smoke - articles of furniture cast away, as of no value to the houseless - and a few domestic fowls, scraping for food among the hills of ashes, were the only objects that told us of man. A few days had sufficed to change a countryside, teeming with the cheeriest sounds of rural life, into a desert." (Balmires)

Bibliography

"Ardnamurchan Settlement, With Blackhouse." Am Baile, uploaded by Am Baile, taken by Mary Ethel Muir Donaldson, 1920-1930, www.ambaile.org.uk/asset/9953/1. Inverness Museum and Art Gallery, Inverness, UK

Blamires, Steve. "The Highland Clearances - an Introduction." Clannada Na Gadelica - Gaelic Traditioalist Resource Site, www.clannada.org/highland6.html.

Cullen, Karen (2010). Famine in Scotland: The "Ill Years" of the 1690s. Edinburgh University Press.

Day, Lorna Corall. "Kelp, Clearances, Clanranald, Speculators and Scottish Scoundrel Lairds." Lenathehyena's Blog, 4 Jan. 2020, lenathehyena.wordpress.com/2019/02/01/kelp-clearances-clanranald-speculators-and-scottish-scoundrel-lairds.

Dimond, Harvey. Entangled Histories: The Highland Clearances and the Transatlantic Slave Trade | Art UK. 19 Jan. 2024, artuk.org/discover/stories/entangled-histories-the-highland-clearances-and-the-transatlantic-slave-trade.

Dreid. "The Secret Symbols of the Jacobites." Culloden Battlefield, 31 July 2015, cullodenbattlefield.wordpress. com/2015/07/31/the-secret-symbols-of-the-jacobites.

Harrison, Marie. "Scotland's Forests Then and Now: Rewilding Scotland - Scotland Magazine." Scotland Mag, uploaded by Scotland Magazine, 20 May 2020, www.scotlandmag.com/ forests-then-and-now-rewilding-scotland.

Henton, Kirsten. "Heresy, They Say? James VI and the Witch Trials - Scotland Magazine." Scotland Magazine, uploaded by Scotland Magazine, 14 Aug. 2020, www.scotlandmag. com/james-vi-and-witch-trials.

"Highland Clearances." Crann Tara, cranntara.scot/clear.htm.

Innes, Ewan J., MA. ScottishHistory.com. 1991, www. scottishhistory.com/articles/highlands/clearances/ clearance_page1.html.

MacInnes, Allan I. (1988). "Scottish Gaeldom: The First Phase of Clearance". In Devine, T M; Mitchison, Rosalind (eds.). People and Society in Scotland, Volume 1, 1760–1830. Edinburgh: John Donald Publishers Ltd.

Mackinlay, James Murray. Folklore of Scottish Lochs and Springs. 1893.

Mackenzie, Alexander, F. S. A. The History of the Highland Clearances. Second Edition, Altered and Revised, Glasgow, United Kingdom of Great Britain and Northern Ireland, P. J.O'Callaghan, 1883, glendiscovery.com/history_of_the_ highland_clearances.html.

Macleod, Donald. Gloomy Memories of the Highlands. Toronto, Canada, Printed for the author by Thompson, 1857, digital. nls.uk/scotlandspages/timeline/18142.html.

Martin, Lauren. "Scottish Witchcraft Panics Re-examined." Palgrave Macmillan UK eBooks, 2008, pp. 119–43. https://doi.org/10.1057/9780230591400_6.

Marx, Karl. "The Duchess of Sutherland and Slavery." History. Hanover.EDU, 21 Jan. 1853, history.hanover.edu/texts/marx/MARXDS&S.html.

McConville, Ben. "Clearing the Air on the Clearances." The Sons of Scotland, www.thesonsofscotland.co.uk/thehighlandclearances.htm.

McGrath, John. The Cheviot, the Stag and the Black, Black Oil. Methuen Drama, 1981.

Prebble, John. The Highland Clearances. Penguin UK, 1982.

Price, Susan. Of Crofters, Kelp and Iodine. 11 Aug. 2017, the-history-girls.blogspot.com/2017/08/of-crofters-kelp-and-iodine-by-susan.html.

Ross, Calum. "Reviving Heritage Lost to the Clearances." PressReader, 1 Feb. 2018, www.pressreader.com/uk/the-press-and-journal-inverness-highlands-and-islands/20180201/283055529853149.

"Scottish Blackhouse - BME Habitatio." BME Habitatio, 28 May 2020, habitatio.epitesz.bme.hu/en/portfolio/scottish-blackhouse.

Steel, Rhona. "Scottish History: The Highland Clearances." Wilderness Scotland, 11 Apr. 2024, www.wildernessscotland.com/blog/highland-clearances.

Steves, Rick. "Battle of Culloden: The End of Scottish Dreams." Rick Steves Classroom Europe, 2017, classroom.ricksteves.com/videos/battle-of-culloden-the-end-of-scottish-dreams.

Stewart, Terry. "The Highland Clearances." Historic UK, 22 Dec. 2023, www.historic-uk.com/HistoryUK/HistoryofScotland/The-Highland-Clearances.

The National Staff. "Scotland Back in the Day: How the Brutal Atrocities of the Highland Clearances Changed Scotland Forever." The National, 19 July 2016, www.thenational.scot/news/14868553.scotland-back-in-the-day-how-the-brutal-atrocities-of-the-highland-clearances-changed-scotland-forever.

The Scottish Government. "Scotland's Forestry Strategy 2019–2029." The Scottish Government, 12 Mar. 2021, www.gov.scot/publications/scotlands-forestry-strategy-20192029/pages/4.

Author's Note

While I can't tell you Margie's story is a true one, I also can't say it isn't

The story came to me on a train through the Highlands; the first paragraphs were written in a 2am creative frenzy as I lay on a bed in a quaint fishing village at the western edge of the green isle. The next morning, I read it aloud to my husband while we sat on an empty boat crossing the choppy strait. While we traveled that choppy sea, trying to not turn green, I did not know just how much this new story would wreck me. I thought it might turn into a light, sort of 'cute' novella which would allow me to obsess over the beautiful nature of the Scottish Highlands and escape to it in the writing.

When we got home and I became properly homesick for the green island that stole my soul (or gave it back to me, depending on your perspective) I started outlining Margie's story. Pretty quickly I realized it would highlight the relationship between the Scottish people and the land. What if the people loved the land and it loved them back? I jotted down and circled sometime in October 2023.

I had an inkling I would set it during the mass-immigration of the Scots to Appalachia, which I hadn't studied but knew of. After all, my ancestors were among those who left their family land of 600+ years to settle, eventually, in the American sisters of the Highland mountains, where I remain to this day.

Then I studied the Clearances — the Lowland Clearances removed my family, and the Highland Clearances removed my husband's. I read through dozens of articles (which comprise the bibliography of this book). Still, with some of the postmortem tidying work done in situations of colonization for the preservation of imperialism's image, it was difficult to form an image of the emotional impact of these times.

Until I found the poets.

In a web article simply called "The Poetry of the Clearances," I found the voice of the people. I found the poets who personified the mist, who talked of it mourning for her lost sons. They wrote of the mist, who howled upon the mountains as it missed them.

I distinctly remember the chills up my arm as I sat in a coffee shop and read it over and over again. I hadn't known this before, and had never heard the mist referred to as a person. In fact, when Margie first came to me, I thought it was perhaps insensitive — my own creativity making an unwanted translation of a heartbreaking history that did not need my narration.

Now I think that's what I heard on that train in the highlands. When we passed the ferns and tree stumps, mushrooms and moss-capped stones, I think it was the soul of the mist I heard, crying about the heights for her lost children. It was the poets who first gave the mist her soul, and it's the writers, the children of the land, who listen to its call.

"What if the land misses its displaced people?" I scrawled and underlined three times.

What if, indeed.

Displacement is something nearly as old as humanity itself, and its damage has left long-reaching scars. While this story is unapologetically Scottish, I thought often of other lands missing their own people. I thought of the very hills in which I live now, and the Tutelo people displaced from them. I hold the tension that they were cast out by people like my displaced ancestors — the dominoes continue their fall. And at the time I'm writing this note, I am thinking of the 1.5 million Palestinians displaced since October 7th of the same year I wrote this story. I think of the 750,000 displaced in 1947, and the 5.9 million Palestinian people who are registered as refugees (making up a third of the worldwide refugee population).

So, while the mist misses its displaced people,
this story is also for the olive trees,
and the old Moratuck river,
and the sands,
and the mountains,
who miss their own children,
and cry for them about the heights.

197

Here's to the poets who cannot be silenced,
who remind us of the places,
we cannot return.

Chaochail madainn air ar n-òige
Mar an ceò air bhàrr nam beann;
Tha ar càirdean 's ar luchd eòlais
Air am fògradh bhos is thall;
Tha cuid eile dhiubh nach gluais,
Tha an cadal fuar fo'n fhòd,
Bha gun uaill, gun fhuath, gun anntlachd
Anns a' ghleann san robh iad òg.

"The joyous morning of our youth has changed
like the mist on the top of the mountains;
our kinsmen and our acquaintances
are driven away in this country and over the sea;
there are others of them who will not move,
who are in a cold sleep under the turf,
people who were without pride, hatred or malice
in the glen in which they were young."

- Neil MacLeod
(19th century Scottish Gaelic Poet)

Ach tha am fàrdaichean sguaibte
'S an seòmraichean uaine;
Iad fhéin is an gaisge
'Nan cadal fo'n fhòd;
'S tha osag nam fuar bheann
Le h-osnaidhean gruamach
'Gan caoidh mu na cruachan
'S a' luaidh air an glòir.

"But their dwellings are swept
and their rooms green:
they themselves and their heroism
asleep under the turf;
and the breeze of the cold mountains
with its gloomy sighs
laments them about the heights
and speaks of their glory."

- Neil MacLeod
(19th century Scottish Gaelic Poet)

Acknowledgements

This book would not exist without the community who keeps me afloat, who remind me that the pain is only labor pangs. Here's to the midwives who held my hand until this story took breath.

To Paul, who watched me fall in love with the land, and knew the sacred joy would create something beautiful. Who held my tears then, and every day since. Who sacrificed his own time and energy to make this real. And here's to our kids, who cheered me on as I wrote, and gently caress my drafts on the desk. Yes, you can read it -- soon.

To my Mosslings: Sarah, Ester, Amber, Hannah, Bailey, and Ella who fell in love with Margie from her inception, and never let her go. Who listened to the first draft through a grainy Marco Polo feed and were my greatest champions every step of the way. Who cheered for the disability rep of "floppy fingers." Who took me to the gulf to hunt for the words in nighttime bioluminescence. Who celebrated milestones with me over virtual drinks, despite the sea between, and gave a mossy rock to the Nicaraguan rainforest in honor of Margie. And here's to those who followed me back across oceans to cry at misty mornings, run the mountain ridges, and hold vigil in the ruins with me. Who buried bits of their souls beneath the heather beside mine. I will spend my life finding a way to thank you and it will never be enough for teaching me what love feels like.

Special thanks to Amber, my sister, who sat up with me on the late nights of editing so I wouldn't be alone. Who read this book more than anyone else, and took me into the forest when I wasn't able to do it on my own. Thank you for loving this story, and loving me, so wholly.

To my beta readers, who jumped into this story in various phases of completion, and saw it's promise. Who believed in the story of a mist sprite, let it sink into their bones, and showed me how to make it even better.

To my editor, Becky Sweeney, who scooped this story up into her arms and made it shine. Who wasn't afraid of my copious, chaotic research, and made it something beautifully coherent. Who brought real Scottish flavor to the story and its texture. Thank you, for helping me tell it true.

And to Sara Willia, the wonderful illustrator of this edition. Who, despite my insane vision, saw Margie and breathed her to life in a whole new way. Who brainstormed with me late into the night (Scotland time!) reading poetry and crying together. I'm so thankful to this process for the sweet kinship it gave me in you.

Here's to all the neighbors, friends, and family who believed in this story, because you believed in me. What wild grace.

And finally, here's to you, reader, for following me into the glen, and making room in your soul for an ancient mist sprite and her grief. Here's to home, and finding it wherever we are.